Praise for the **Whole Nother Story** series

An IndieBound Next Pick
A *Kirkus Reviews* Best Children's Book of the Year
An Al Roker *Today Show* Book Club Pick

★ "A grand escapade centered around a close family of smart, helpful, likable characters who run into all sorts of oddball wanderers." —*Kirkus Reviews*, starred review

"My favorite part? The WHOLE BOOK!" —Kent, a kid

"A magnificent adventure [that] kids will want to read . . . over and over again." —Kidsreads.com

"If you take yourself very seriously, perhaps this isn't the book for you. But if you're in the mood for a lot of silliness and reading about a really interesting and quirky family, then it's perfect." —Wired.com/GeekDad

"[A] fast-paced adventure." —*Publishers Weekly*

"Rip-roaring. . . . The laugh-out-loud moments are many." —*SLJ*

"THIS BOOK ROCKS!" —Rose, another kid

Books by the one and only
DR. CUTHBERT SOUP

A Whole Nother Story
Another Whole Nother Story
No Other Story

NO OTHER STORY

Dr. Cuthbert Soup

illustrations by

Jeffrey Stewart Timmins

BLOOMSBURY
NEW YORK LONDON NEW DELHI SYDNEY

First published in the United States of America in September 2012
by Bloomsbury Children's Books
Paperback edition published in September 2013
www.bloomsbury.com

For information about permission to reproduce selections from this book, write to
Permissions, Bloomsbury Children's Books, 1385 Broadway, New York, New York 10018
Bloomsbury books may be purchased for business or promotional use. For information on bulk
purchases please contact Macmillan Corporate and Premium Sales Department at
specialmarkets@macmillan.com

The Library of Congress has cataloged the hardcover edition as follows:
Soup, Cuthbert.
No other story / by Dr. Cuthbert Soup.
p.   cm.
Sequel to: Another whole nother story.
Summary: When Mr. Cheeseman and his three smart, polite, and relatively
odor-free children journey to the not-so-distant past, they meet something
utterly surprising—the alternate versions of themselves.
ISBN 978-1-59990-824-3 (hardcover)
[1. Time travel—Fiction. 2. Inventions—Fiction.
3. Family life—Fiction. 4. Humorous stories.] I. Title.
PZ7.S7249No 2012   [Fic]—dc23   2012009589

ISBN 978-1-61963-120-5 (paperback)

Book design by Donna Mark
Typeset by Westchester Book Composition
Printed and bound in the U.S.A. by Thomson-Shore Inc., Dexter, Michigan
2 4 6 8 10 9 7 5 3 1

All papers used by Bloomsbury Publishing, Inc., are natural, recyclable products
made from wood grown in well-managed forests. The manufacturing processes
conform to the environmental regulations of the country of origin.

For Sir Finley the Dimpled

FIGHT ILLITERACY.
GIVE TO YOUR LOCAL LIBERRY.

"It takes two to tango, but it takes four to tango with a giant squid."

DR. CUTHBERT SOUP, ADVISOR TO THE ILL-ADVISED

A BIT OF ADVICE

Though I have never been on the run from government agents, international superspies, or corporate villains, I can certainly identify with Ethan Cheeseman and his three smart, polite, attractive, and relatively odor-free children. You see, when I was growing up, my father was in the army, so we were constantly moving from town to town because he was a deserter.

Thankfully, those days are over; for me, but not for the Cheesemans, who are still on the run as we speak, and I don't envy them one bit. Well, except for the fact that they now have access to a fully operational time machine, and what could be more exciting than that? There are so many great times throughout history that one might wish to visit. Last Tuesday was a very nice day, for instance. And just imagine being able to go back in time and shake hands with Abraham Lincoln, or take a ride on a woolly mammoth, or, if the opportunity were to present itself, take a ride on Abraham Lincoln. (Not without asking first, as that would be rude.)

Of course, the Cheesemans have no immediate desire to ride on extinct mammals or, for that matter, extinct presidents. And last Tuesday, though the weather was quite agreeable, holds very little interest for them. They have one use and one use only for the time machine, and that is to save the life of Olivia Cheeseman, Ethan's lovely wife and mother to his children. They intend to do this by traveling back to the time before she was poisoned by the evilest of villains and preventing said villain from carrying out his heinous crime.

However, this is much easier said than done. Though the LVR-ZX has been proven to be quite capable of transporting humans along the Time Arc, there are still many problems to work out with this new technology. In short, perfecting time travel will take . . . well, time. After all, as the old saying goes, Rome wasn't built in France. (Which is a good thing, considering how much longer it would have taken, having to haul all those fancy statues over the French Alps.)

So before you go getting yourself all lathered up over the possibility of traveling back to ancient Egypt to watch them invent the calendar, or to ancient China to watch them invent spaghetti, or gunpowder, or a gun that shoots spaghetti against the wall to see if it sticks, I would strongly suggest that you first read this book as a cautionary tale of some of the horrible problems that might await you.

CHAPTER 1

You could see their reflections getting smaller as they moved quickly away from the shiny, metallic surface of the football-shaped LVR-ZX and across the seemingly endless field of dry grass, sparsely decorated with the occasional wildflower or aimlessly flitting butterfly.

The mood was light and joyous, for they were, to a person, quite happy to be rid of the year 1668 and back to being somewhere close to the present. The children were especially happy for two reasons:

1. After what seemed like a lifetime of being on the run, each day wondering if they might never see her alive again, they would finally have the chance to embrace their mother once more.
2. There's no time like the present.

Professor Boxley was perhaps slightly less happy than the rest of the group, but that was only due to the fact that his lungs felt like a balloon that had been bent, stretched,

3

and twisted into the shape of a poodle by a circus clown. The old man hadn't done any running in years, and he now found himself bent at the waist, clutching at and leaning on his bony kneecaps, in an effort to keep his red, puffy face from meeting the ground below.

"Hold on, everybody," said Mr. Cheeseman, the first to notice the professor had fallen out. He jogged back and placed his hand on his former teacher's back. "Are you okay, Professor?"

Professor Boxley tottered briefly under the extra weight of Ethan's hand, then responded by holding up a single finger, as if to say, "I would love to answer that question once I regain my breath. Check back in a week or so."

Ethan quickly removed his jacket and spread it out on the ground. By the time he had done so, his three children, Chip Krypton, Penny Nickelton, and Teddy Roosevelt, had run back to help. They took the wheezing senior citizen beneath his shaky arms and lowered him to a sitting position on the jacket.

You may be wondering why it is that the Cheeseman children all went by different last names; the answer is quite simple. Each time over the past two years that Pinky, the Cheesemans' psychic, hairless fox terrier, warned them of impending danger, they packed up everything they owned, moved to a new location, and, for added protection against evil villains, changed their names, first and last.

Ethan allowed his children to be as creative as they wanted when it came to choosing their new names. While some parents might worry that encouraging a child's creativity could lead to them just making stuff up all the time—two plus two equals Benjamin Franklin, for instance—Ethan was of the mind that young imaginations should never be harnessed, and I couldn't agree more. After all, who would want to grow up in a world where two plus two always equals John Quincy Adams?

"I'm sorry," said the professor, when he had finally gathered enough breath to do so. "I think the heat just got to me. I guess I'm not as young as I used to be."

"You're not as old as you used to be, either," said eight-year-old Teddy, the youngest and most outspoken of Ethan's children.

Penny glared at Teddy the way she always did when he spat out an insensitive remark. "Try something new, Teddy," she said. "Like thinking before you speak. For once."

As Teddy saw it, the worst thing about being the youngest member of a family was that everyone, it seemed, thought it entirely within their rights to boss him around. "What?" he protested. "I'm just saying that he's from fifteen years in the future, so, right now, he's a lot younger than he was before."

"Makes sense to me," added Gravy-Face Roy, Teddy's equally outspoken sock puppet. Gravy-Face Roy was actually nothing more than an old tube sock perched upon Teddy's left arm and decorated with two eyes and a nose made of greasy beef-gravy stains.

As you might imagine, those beefy splotches made

Gravy-Face Roy very attractive to Pinky, who smacked her lips whenever the loudmouth sock puppet came within smelling distance.

"I don't think it works that way," said Penny. Out of habit, she went to toss her long auburn hair over her shoulder, only to be reminded that she had chopped most of it off, leaving it back in the seventeenth century. This had not been an easy thing for her to do, for the simple fact that her hair reminded her so much of her beloved mother; each day she washed it with a special shampoo made of wheat germ, honey, strawberry, coconut, apple pectin, pineapple, and Canadian bacon.

If you were to ask Mr. Cheeseman about the scientific benefits of such a concoction, he would most likely tell you that in order for food to be helpful to your hair, you must actually eat it. After all, carrots are good for your eyes, but not if you apply them directly. Likewise, fish is said to be brain food, but rubbing a mackerel on your head will only result in the loss of friends and possibly some unwanted attention from hungry seagulls.

"Just because the professor traveled back in time to rescue us doesn't mean his physical age changes," Penny continued. "By your logic, while we were all back in 1668, we were hundreds of years younger than we are now, and that would be impossible."

"I guess you're right," Teddy relented. Gravy-Face Roy nodded in agreement. After all, who were they to argue with the brilliant Penny Nickelton, who had an IQ of 164 and an RQ of 2047?

What is an *RQ*, you ask? I would explain it, but it's something that can only be understood by people with an IQ of 160 or greater, and if you have an IQ this high, then you already know what an RQ is.

It was certainly no great secret where Penny got her smarts. Her mother had been a world-class mathematician, and her father was one of the greatest inventors the world has ever known. In fact, by the time Ethan had graduated from Southwestern North Dakota State University, the handsome, bespectacled genius had been credited with the following scientific breakthroughs:

- Fat-free lard.
- Sour cream and onion–flavored dental floss.
- Solar-powered musical pants.
- The Monkey Mobile.*

Of course, Ethan's greatest work was done in the area of time travel and the development of the LVR, the world's first working time machine. Unfortunately, the Cheesemans had been forced to leave the LVR back in 1668 when it was badly damaged in a crash landing. As luck would have it, however, Professor Boxley was able to launch a rescue mission from fifteen years into the future with his own LVR-ZX, a machine patterned after the one designed by his former star student, Ethan Cheeseman.

---

*The Monkey Mobile was an automobile that ran entirely on monkey sweat and created absolutely no air pollution (unless you consider the smell of sweaty monkeys to be a pollutant).

"Okay," said the professor, with a sharp exhale. "I think I'm good to go. As long as we slow the pace down a bit, if you don't mind."

"Sorry about that," said Chip. "We were just excited to see her again." He smiled, and his patchy teenage mustache spread out across his upper lip, thinning it further so that it was every bit as full as a baby's eyebrow.

"Hey, Dad," said Teddy, "after we save Mom, can we all go out for ice cream, like we used to?"

"You bet we can," said Ethan.

As Chip and Ethan helped the professor to his feet, Teddy looked to the sky and saw something rather strange; something none of them had noticed before. Just moments ago, when they all stepped out of the LVR-ZX with no idea whether they had made it back to their own time or not, it was a very modern jet airplane rumbling across the sky that provided solid evidence that they had succeeded.

"That's weird," said Teddy as he casually blew a small bubble with the stale gum he'd been gnawing on. Teddy was a habitual gum chewer and, though not widely publicized, at nine weeks, four days, six hours, and twenty-three minutes, he held the unofficial record for continually chewing something completely and utterly without flavor.

When the others looked up, they also saw what Teddy had determined to be weird. On most occasions, one wouldn't be terribly surprised to look up and see the moon, being that *up* is where the moon is normally located. However, this was the middle of the day.

Indeed, there are times when the moon shows itself during daylight hours, but usually only partially, and rather faintly at that. But this moon was bright and full and the sky surrounding it was dark, even though the sun shone brightly above. There were even a few flickering stars.

"You're right, Teddy," said Ethan, his forehead wrinkled with confusion and concern. "That *is* weird."

Teddy very much enjoyed being right (it didn't happen all that often), and he was looking forward to basking in the warm glow of rightness when an odd sound rose up from beyond a nearby hill. As it grew louder, it could soon be identified as drumming, and mixed with that drumming was the sound of a flute or a fife or some kind of a flute-fife combo.

"Sounds like a parade," said Chip, squinting into the bright sun-moon-starlight.

In no time, it not only sounded like a parade, but looked like one as well when row after row of men came marching over the hill, led by three others on horseback. The men marched with rifles perched upon their shoulders. But these weren't just any rifles—the rifles the men carried appeared to be very new-looking antique rifles, and their uniforms bore a striking resemblance to those worn by soldiers of the American Revolution.

"Hmm," said Teddy. "Not much of a parade. No floats, no clowns, no giant balloons shaped like SpongeBob."

"Maybe they're on their way to join a bigger parade," Chip offered.

"Yes," said Penny hopefully. "Since we don't know the exact date, it's possible that it's July 4th and they're on their way to march in an Independence Day parade."

"Could be," said Mr. Cheeseman. "Either way, they've got to be going somewhere. Maybe they can help us find the nearest town."

"Or some cotton candy," said Teddy.

Pinky said nothing. This is just another advantage of having a psychic dog. If the dog growls, you know that danger is afoot. Likewise, a lack of growling will tell you that all is well, allowing you to save all that angst for times when there's actually something to worry about. "You kids go ahead," said Ethan. "Professor Boxley and I will be along shortly."

The soldiers marched quickly and with purpose, and catching them wasn't all that easy. Chip was the first to reach them, which was not surprising, being that he was a natural athlete and a formidable baseball pitcher who could throw the following pitches with great accuracy: sinker, slider, fastball, curveball, screwball, forkball, knuckleball, and forkleball (a wicked knuckleball-forkball combo).

"Excuse me," shouted Chip over the sounds of drumming, fluting, and marching as he sidled up to one of the drummers at the rear of the regiment. The round-faced boy appeared to be no older than twelve, and Chip thought he looked tired, lugging around that heavy drum. Beads of sweat streamed down his face and clung to the tip of his nose. "Sorry to bother you."

"No bother at all," said the boy. "Name's Cheeks, on account of I got a chubby face. What's yours?"

"I'm Chip. I was just wondering where you're headed."

"On our way to fight the Romans," said Cheeks, taking care not to fall out of step with the rest of the marchers.

"Romans?" said Penny, who was quite athletic herself and had arrived on the scene just seconds after Chip. "I think you mean the British."

"What I mean is what I said," Cheeks remarked flatly. "Marched all day from Charlestown to intercept the Romans. Too much, if you ask me. I'm thinking of putting in for a transfer to a different regiment."

"Well, if I were you, I would put in for a transfer to a different school," said Penny. "One that teaches proper history."

"No time for school," said Cheeks. "Too busy fighting the Romans."

"That's ridiculous," Penny scoffed as Teddy ran up and immediately began admiring Cheeks's drum and the boy's proficiency with it, or at least how loudly he was able to bang on it.

"It's ridiculous all right," said Cheeks. "All this fighting. And if it's not the Romans, it's the Huns."

Penny practically fell over. "The Huns? You may think you're being funny, but you're actually proving yourself to be nothing more than an ignoramus." Cheeks responded by giving Penny a rather dirty look.

"You shouldn't call people names," said Teddy with a smack of his gum.

"You don't even know what it means," snapped Penny.

"I do so," Teddy shot back. "An ignoramus is . . . a type of dinosaur."

"Amazing," said Penny. "You're exactly right. You must be some kind of genius. Now, do you know what *sarcastic* means?"

"Nooo," said Teddy sarcastically.

"Come on," said Chip. "Don't you think you're being a little hard on him?"

Just because Penny was the owner of a genius-level IQ doesn't mean she wasn't wrong from time to time. This was one of those times. She sighed and placed her hand on Teddy's shoulder. "I'm sorry, Teddy. I'm sorry I lost my patience with you. But the sooner we find out where we are, the sooner we can find Mom."

"I know," said Teddy. "It's okay."

Just then, a commotion rose up from the front of the ranks. There was much yelling, and the men quite suddenly stopped marching. This allowed Ethan and the professor to catch up to the others.

"What's going on?" asked Mr. Cheeseman. "Did you find out where they're headed?"

"The drummer told us they're on their way to fight the Romans," said Chip.

"Romans?" echoed the professor. He stroked his bristly white mustache and his face took on a look of consternation.

The men on horseback barked out orders as the soldiers quickly formed two very long lines, one in front of the other. They removed their rifles from their shoulders and began loading them with lead balls and powder.

Pinky growled, low and steadily.

"What's going on?" asked Teddy in his most panicky voice.

"I don't know," said Penny, becoming anxious herself. "I can't see anything."

"Vikings," said Cheeks with a sigh of disgust. "Can you believe it?"

"No, as a matter of fact, I can't believe it," said Penny. "In fact, if you told me the sky was blue, I'd get a second opinion." But when she and the others looked beyond the soldiers to the horizon up ahead, they realized that Cheeks was right. Amassed along the crest of a nearby hill was a group of men, perhaps two hundred in number, dressed in animal skins and wearing helmets adorned with goat and steer horns. Like an angry mob, the unruly men assaulted the air with a wave of obscenities shouted in their ancient Viking dialect. They waved their swords, axes, and large, circular shields, and, though you should never judge a book by its cover, if these men were books, you can bet they could stink up a library real good. (Or a liberry, for that matter.)

"Well," said Gravy-Face Roy. "Maybe it's Viking Independence Day too."

"I don't like the looks of this," said Mr. Cheeseman, who, like Professor Boxley, was beginning to suspect the worst.

"Tell me about it," said Cheeks. "Looks like they got us

outnumbered, two to one. It ain't gonna be pretty, that's for sure."

Of the two lines of soldiers, the line in front dropped to one knee on command from one of the horsemen, who drew his sword from its scabbard and thrust it skyward. The soldiers in the second line remained standing.

"Ready!" shouted the horseman, his sword gleaming in the sun- and moonlight. The soldiers in both lines placed the butts of their rifles against their shoulders.

"Aim!" In unison, they closed one eye and brought the other close to their gun sights. Though Ethan and his children had never before found themselves in the middle of a battle, they had all seen enough movies to know what came next. There was no such thing as "Ready! Aim! Dance!" or "Ready! Aim! Knit a sweater!" In battle there was only one thing that came next, and it definitely did seem as though a battle was about to break out. If it was merely a historical reenactment, it was not a very historically accurate one.

The Vikings let out a collective yell that raised the hair on the back of Teddy's neck and the cotton on the back of Gravy-Face Roy's. They took off running toward the soldiers, maniacally and without fear or reason. Teddy clung to his father's leg. Penny found Chip's hand and clenched it tightly. Pinky growled again and wedged herself between Ethan's ankles.

Then, just as the commanding officer was about to yell "Dance!"—wait, sorry. Just as he was about to yell "Fire!" a savage roar split the air. The once-fearless Vikings stopped in their tracks. The horses flared their nostrils and reared up, nearly throwing their riders to the ground. Pinky growled and barked.

"Retreat!" yelled the commander of the minutemen.

The Viking leader must have yelled something similar, because, just as quickly as they had appeared, the smelly-looking warriors turned and ran back the way they had come, while the soldiers took off in the opposite direction.

"Better run too," said Cheeks. "Unless you wanna be lunch. Trust me. Those things are awfully nasty creatures."

The Cheesemans and the professor wanted to run, but they were awestruck to the point of paralysis by what they saw next. With another deafening roar, an enormous prehistoric beast, its teeth glistening with saliva in the sun-moon-starlight, emerged from behind the tree line.

"I don't believe it," said the professor.

"It's a dinosaur," said Chip.

"It's an ignoramus," said Teddy.

The dinosaur, with a brain the size of a grapefruit, may very well have been an ignoramus, but it was also a Tyrannosaurus rex. Ethan and the others watched helplessly as the enormous beast lumbered over to the LVR-ZX and gave it a good sniff.

The humongous animal was apparently in need of a meal and, upon a second look, some serious dental work. It goes without saying this was the first T. rex that Mr. Cheeseman and the others had ever encountered in person. However, they had seen plenty of pictures in books and reconstructed specimens in museums, and this was the only one they'd seen with such a severe overbite. That's right—this particular T. rex had buckteeth. And not just buckteeth—gnarled, snarled, misaligned, nasty-looking buck- teeth that shot out in all directions. Imagine, if you will, a picket fence after a hurricane.

Its unfortunate dental work made the dinosaur look like a dimwit, or, if you prefer, an ignoramus. But was it as stupid as it looked? The creature answered the question by kicking at the LVR-ZX, then, perhaps mistaking the egg- shaped vessel for an egg-shaped egg, opened its snaggle- toothed mouth and clamped its massive jaws around the time machine's metallic outer shell.

"Oh no," whispered Penny. "Should we try to stop him?"

"How?" asked Chip. "Look at the size of him. He's like a gas station with teeth."

"He's like a gas station with really *bad* teeth," said Teddy.

With a heart-sinking, hope-dashing crunch, the LVR-ZX collapsed under the pressure of the dopey-looking ani- mal's massive jaws. When this failed to bring the desired result (a dinosaur-egg omelet, one can only assume), the T. rex dropped the machine to the ground and began stomp- ing it with its gigantic feet, until the LVR-ZX was as flat as a garbage-can lid. The battered time machine was now about as useful as a tennis racket at a banjo recital. (If you've ever been to a banjo recital, you know exactly what I mean; if you've never been to a banjo recital, consider yourself lucky.)

Ethan stood with his mouth agape. His face had lost all color. "I was afraid of this," he said. "It looks as though we're in Some Times."

"Yes," agreed the professor. "And it looks as though we're here permanently."

SOME TIMELY ADVICE

In late June of 1776, Thomas Jefferson completed his first draft of the Declaration of Independence. He was then ordered to write a second draft when the Continental Congress found the first one to be "just plain not funny." The much punchier second draft was adopted by Congress on July 4th, which just so happened to coincide perfectly with the young nation's annual fireworks display. And so, for the next seven years, England would wage war with the American colonists, a group of patriots lured to combat by the promise of freedom and triangular hats.

They engaged in many fierce battles, including the one at Bunker Hill, where Colonel William Prescott is said to have ordered, "Don't fire until you see the whites of their eyes." The crafty redcoats handed the patriots a sound defeat by coming in squinting.

Eventually, as we all know, the Americans would emerge victorious, in part because they did not have to worry about Romans, Huns, Vikings, dinosaurs, Vikings riding on dinosaurs, or dinosaurs riding on Vikings. They did not have to worry because, at that time, none of those things existed. It is a scientific fact that humans did not live in the time of dinosaurs, and it's a good thing, because dinosaur names are so long that, by the time one human warned another that one of these creatures was sneaking up behind him, that person would be what dinosaurs commonly referred to as a *tasty snack treat.*

"Look out, Stig [very common caveman name]! There's a Pachycephalosaurus right behind . . . uh, never mind."

Therefore, if you ever find yourself face-to-face with a dinosaur while at the same time hanging out with American colonial soldiers and Vikings, there's a very good chance that you might have been bumped off the Time Arc, landing in a place known to the scientific community as Some Times, where day and night, January and August, the Dark Ages and the Age of Enlightenment can all be happening at once.

If you suspect that this may be the case, I advise you to return to your time machine immediately and get the heck out of there. Otherwise you may find yourself watching Fourth of July fireworks on Christmas morning, which, if you ask me, would be just plain not funny.

CHAPTER 2

The great Albert Einstein once said, "I'll give ten dollars to anyone who refers to me as great." *Cha-ching!* He also said some other stuff, such as, "The only reason for time is so that everything doesn't happen at once."

In that awful, mysterious, and awfully mysterious place known as Some Times, that's exactly what's happening. Everything. At once.

"My LVR-ZX," muttered Professor Boxley with despair, his mustache quivering. "It's been completely destroyed."

For a person willing to take the risk of traveling along the highly unpredictable Time Arc, the professor was, to put it politely, a bit of a timid sort, and to put it impolitely, a coward. His knees buckled slightly, and he latched on to Teddy's shoulder to steady himself.

"Are you okay, Professor?" asked Chip.

"I think I peed my pants a little," said the professor sheepishly, although it should be noted that sheep rarely wet their pants, because they are generally not great believers in the wearing of trousers. Teddy said nothing, but casually stepped away from the professor, leaving the old man with his dampened pants to stand on his own.

"I don't understand," said Penny. "What's going on?"

"Some Times," said Mr. Cheeseman, with a dispassionate stare. "Up until now it was regarded as only a theory. But I'd say we now have definite proof of its existence."

"So then . . ." Penny began to say what everyone was thinking but none of them wanted to hear. "We didn't make it back after all."

Ethan's neck bowed under the weight of his head, heavy with sadness and with the guilt of knowing he had failed his children once again. "No," he concurred. "We didn't make it back. But we will. Somehow."

"Okay, let me get this straight," said Chip. "Are you saying we discovered Some Times?"

"It would appear so," said Ethan.

"This is huge," he said with enthusiasm, trying to get the rest of the group to look on the bright side. "It's kind of like finding Atlantis. We'll be famous."

"Only if we live to tell about it," said Ethan.

"What does that mean?" asked Teddy. "Are you saying we're going to die?" He chomped his gum with something close to violence, as he always did when overcome by nervousness.

"Not if we're smart," Ethan said. He placed his hand on the back of Teddy's neck and gave it a reassuring squeeze that was slightly less reassuring than Teddy would have liked.

The T. rex, now entirely convinced that the LVR-ZX was

not something good to eat, seemed intent on finding something that was. It raised its head and appeared to be sniffing at the air, its twisted choppers dripping copious amounts of thick saliva.

"There is some debate as to the land speed of a Tyrannosaurus rex," said Penny. "It is estimated to be anywhere between eleven and forty-five miles per hour."

"That's quite a disparity," said Professor Boxley.

"What's the land speed of people?" asked Teddy.

"Depends on which people you're talking about," said Mr. Cheeseman, surveying the group, which included a frightened elderly man, an eight-year-old boy, and a short-legged dog. "Either way, I suggest we get moving. Before he moves on to plan B. [The *B* presumably standing for *brunch*.] Let's go." Chip took the lead and the others followed, sprinting through the grassy field.

Most dinosaurs are classified as reptiles, and, in general, reptiles are not known to have terribly good eyesight. Snakes, for instance, have such poor vision that they must find their way around with their tongues, which I would not recommend unless you live in a house made of bacon. Unfortunately for the Cheesemans, however, the T. rex was an exception to the bad eyesight rule, and, scanning the open field, it noticed something moving. No, it noticed some *things* moving; some things that, to the T. rex, must have looked like strips of crispy bacon on two legs (or, in the case of Pinky, four legs).

With another bone-chilling roar, the goofy-looking lizard king took off after the human snack treats, pounding the earth with its massive feet. The situation appeared bleak at best. The grassy plain provided no cover and no chance of escape. It seemed a foregone conclusion that one or all of them would be killed at the hands (tiny though they might be) of the much faster T. rex.

"Dad," yelled Chip, "I think I can outrun him. I can lead him away so you guys can escape." Of course, deep down, Chip knew he had very little chance of outrunning the monster, but the thought of the T. rex wiping out his entire family made him more courageous than he otherwise might have been.

"No," said Mr. Cheeseman. "We stay together as a family. No matter what happens."

They ran for the hilltop, hoping to find something on the other side that might give them a chance, but what that something might be, they hadn't a clue.

A glance over his shoulder let Mr. Cheeseman know that the beast was getting closer with each passing moment. At the same time, Professor Boxley was getting farther away. The old man's legs appeared rubbery, and his face was the color of a grape; the red kind, not the green. He stumbled and regained his balance, but only for a moment before crashing to the ground.

Ethan ran back to his friend and tried to pull him to a standing position as the T. rex closed the gap by twenty feet with each enormous stride. "Come on, Professor. Get up!"

"Please. I'm too young to die," blubbered the seventy-year-old professor.

"You'll be okay," said Ethan. "Now take my hand!"

The children heard the commotion over the dinosaur's relentless pounding of the ground and ran back to help. "No," said Ethan. "Keep going!"

"You said we stay together as a family, no matter what," shouted Penny. With the children's help, Ethan was able to hoist the professor into an upright position, and together the four of them helped the exhausted and terrified old man to stagger across the last remaining feet to the top of the small hill. By now they could almost feel the hot breath of the cold-blooded killer as it continued to surge closer and closer.

When they finally reached the top of the hill, they would have been shocked at what lay on the other side if they'd had time to stop and comprehend it. It wasn't so much *what* it was that they saw, but *when* it was. And the when that it was, was winter; freezing, cold, everything-covered-with-snow winter. Moving from summer to winter with one tiny step is something that one can only do in Some Times, or, perhaps, while touring a Popsicle factory.

The scene before them was not a welcome sight. No Popsicles, just deep snow that was sure to slow them down even further, allowing the T. rex to catch up in no time and gobble them all up with its multidirectional teeth. Clad in jeans, T-shirts, and light jackets, none of them was prepared for the cold. Still, with no other choice, they staggered down the steep, slippery hill toward the valley below.

For a moment, Ethan thought that perhaps the T. rex would not follow them. After all, hadn't some scientists theorized that the Ice Age had killed the dinosaurs? His momentary glimmer of hope faded with the sun as the towering creature's shadow fell over them. Undeterred by the freezing temperatures, the T. rex stepped from summer to winter and lumbered down the hill after them.

"Dad!" yelled Penny.

"Keep running," Ethan implored. The deep snow was too much for Teddy's short legs, and Mr. Cheeseman scooped up his spiky-haired son without missing a beat. Likewise, Pinky found herself struggling through the frozen fluff. Chip plucked the hairless terrier up and tucked her beneath his arm like a four-legged football. He fully realized that each awkward step he took could be his last. It would take a miracle to save them now.

Another roar rose up from behind them. But this roar sounded different. This was not the sound of a hungry T. rex; this was a low, rolling roar that built slowly and spread across the ground like an earthquake. By way of its massive feet repeatedly pounding the frozen earth, the T. rex had started an avalanche. Not exactly the miracle Ethan and the others had been hoping for.

The tremendous swell of snow suddenly made the T. rex look much smaller than before as it raced down from above. When the snow caught up with the dinosaur, the force of the powdery wall knocked the beast off its feet. It fell like an ancient redwood, its oversized head colliding with the ground a mere ten feet behind Mr. Cheeseman and drenching him with thick, slimy, prehistoric spit. The surge of snow and ice swept over and around the fallen creature and toward the dinosaur's human prey.

Their minds raced with the awful possibilities that awaited them. Would it be preferable to be eaten by a humongous lizard or to be buried alive beneath a surging mountain of snow? Not much of a choice, but at least with the avalanche they had a chance for survival; and there was only one way to survive an avalanche. Ethan knew exactly what it was.

"Swim!" he shouted as the racing mass of white scooped them up and carried them off like a powerful tidal wave. And so they swam. In a furious, desperate crawl stroke for life, they kicked their legs and spun their arms and hoped for the best.

CHAPTER 3

It's strange, the things that race through your mind when you're staring death in the face. Events from your past, things you've done, things you forgot to do, things you wish you hadn't done, and myriad faces, places, and images that piece together your entire life. One of the faces that made an appearance in Chip's mind was that of his first and only love, the pretty girl named Big, whom he had been forced to leave back in the seventeenth century. He hoped to return to her one day, but that possibility appeared far less likely now that he was stuck in Some Times, plummeting down a steep hill along with two tons of snow and eight tons of dinosaur.

The images that made their way into Teddy's brain included the soft, kind face of his mother and the soft, woolly face of Steve, the sock puppet she had knitted for him before she passed away; the same sock puppet Pinky had torn apart with her sharp fox terrier teeth. Gravy-Face Roy had proven adequate as a temporary replacement, but if Teddy was ever so lucky as to see his mother again, he fully intended to ask her to knit him an exact replica of the original Steve.

Penny saw her mother as well. But this was not just a random image pulled up from her expansive memory bank. You see, Penny had a history of encounters with ghosts and other apparitions, and this, it seemed, was yet another. This time, Olivia appeared to be floating weightlessly in the middle of a snowstorm. And though the weather raged all around her, she seemed completely unaffected by it. Her smile was soft and perfect, her hair sleek and fiery with not a single strand out of place. Her lips parted, and in a reassuring, almost melodic tone, she said, "Face the music, face the facts, back to front and hurry back."

As always, these brushes Penny had with the supernatural made no sense whatsoever. But before Penny could ask her mother the meaning of the enigmatic poem, Olivia was enveloped by the swirling snow and carried off on the breeze, leaving Penny alone in her fight for survival.

As a scientist, it is no surprise that the things speeding through Ethan's head were of a more technical nature. One of the stranger notions that occurred to him as he found himself completely surrounded by billions of tiny snowflakes, all acting in concert to smother him, was that each of those snowflakes was slightly different from the others. Of the countless number of flakes that have ever existed, no two have ever been exactly alike. Snowflakes are unique, just like fingerprints, which means there is nothing quite so unique in the universe as a snowman's fingerprints.

What occupied the space between Professor Boxley's ears was a nagging regret and a very strong feeling that the middle of winter is perhaps the worst possible time to wet one's pants.

Though the images that filled their heads seemed to encompass a lifetime, they actually lasted for only a matter of seconds before the raucous din of sliding snow and ice finally subsided, giving way to an eerie silence. Teddy opened his eyes and was pleased to find that the avalanche was over, and even more pleased to find that his life was not. He tugged and tugged and finally extracted his left leg from the snow bank. He pulled himself to his feet and was happy to see Penny sitting in front of him.

"Where is everyone?" he asked.

This was a question Penny could not answer because her face, at that moment, was covered with snow. When she had wiped it away, her frozen lips became immediately contorted in shock and fear. "T-t-t-teddy," she stuttered while looking just beyond him. Teddy spun around and found himself staring right into the gigantic eye of the T. rex. With its tiny arms, the dinosaur was not a good swimmer, and was now buried up to its neck in snow.

"Look," said Teddy. "He can't move."

"Ha!" taunted Gravy-Face Roy. "You don't scare us anymore."

"I wouldn't do that if I were you," said Penny.

The T. rex responded to Gravy-Face Roy's relentless teasing with a vicious growl. It not only scared Teddy and his handmade sock puppet, but the resulting wind lifted them off the ground and sent them careening farther down the hill in a tangled mass of arms, legs, and gravy-stained sock. The force also blew a large mound of snow aside, and lying there beneath it were Professor Boxley and Chip, with Pinky still cradled in his arms like a football. Despite the enormous impact of the avalanche, Chip had not fumbled the dog. The three of them sat up, stunned and gasping for air.

Chip nearly leaped out of his frozen pants when he saw the dinosaur's head just feet away, its teeth like jagged, twisted stalactites, dripping with saliva. It roared again, and the force knocked Chip backward and temporarily straightened his curly black hair.

"It's okay," said Penny. "He's stuck in the snow. He can't hurt us now."

"Yes," the professor muttered. "But this is Some Times. For all we know, spring could be just minutes away. Then what?"

"Then we'd better get out of here before he thaws out," said Chip. "Where's Dad?"

"I don't know," said Teddy. "But here's his shoe." Sure enough, not more than a couple of feet from where Teddy sat in the snow was a size ten-and-a-half brown shoe, belonging to none other than Ethan Cheeseman. But when Teddy crawled over and tried to lift the shoe, it wouldn't budge. This was most likely due to the fact that Mr. Cheeseman was still in it. Teddy pulled harder on the shoe and off it came, revealing a sock-covered foot. This is one instance in which being up to one's ankles in snow was far more serious than it sounded.

Penny let out a panicky gasp and she and the others immediately sprang into action, clawing frantically at the snow, digging downward.

"Come on, faster!" Chip ordered.

As the humans quickened their pace, Pinky joined the efforts. She had learned much about digging back in the year 1668 from Digs, who was Big's pet fox and an expert hole digger. Pinky now put her newfound knowledge to good use, using her front paws to shovel the snow rapidly between her hind legs just as she had watched the little brown fox do.

When they had dug down to Mr. Cheeseman's waist (or up to his waist, depending on how you look at), Chip and the professor each took a leg and dragged Ethan back to the surface. They placed him on his back, and the children made way for Professor Boxley. Though he was not a medical doctor, the professor knew a great deal more than the rest of them about human physiology. With a trembling hand, he first checked Mr. Cheeseman's pulse, and found it to be slow. *Very* slow.

"How is he?" asked Penny doubtfully, for she had never seen her father looking so lifeless and with such a bluish tint about him. There was a large lump over his left eye where he had collided with something on the way down the hill. The bump left Ethan's eye swollen nearly shut and his battered face scarcely recognizable.

"He's taken quite a blow to the head," said the professor.

"I suspect a concussion and the onset of hypothermia. We've got to get him back up the hill to where it's warm."

It wasn't until then that they realized just how far the avalanche had taken them down the hillside. Looking up, they saw that the journey back to summer would be a long, steep, and slippery climb. Meanwhile, the T. rex continued to roar, each time releasing enough hot breath to melt a little more of the snow that, so far, had held it captive and rendered it harmless; except to their eardrums, which took a pounding whenever the creature opened its cavernous, bucktoothed mouth.

The professor was shaky with exhaustion and fear, so Chip and Penny took their unconscious father beneath his arms and attempted to pull him to an upright position. Despite having a rather severe sweet tooth and a fondness for doughnuts, ice cream, and cake of all kinds, Mr. Cheeseman was not a large man. In fact, he was very much on the thin side. Still, for a fourteen-year-old boy and a twelve-year-old girl, lugging him up a steep, snowy hill would be no easy task, and, indeed, might very well prove impossible.

Their hands were purple. Their fingers were stiff and responded with stubbornness to the task before them. Chip realized he was shivering involuntarily, his bottom molars clacking against the top. Penny's teeth were also chattering, and between the two of them, their mouths sounded like a smattering of applause. Finally, with a little help from Teddy and the professor, Chip and Penny managed to pull their father to something close to a standing position.

They took their first wobbly step as the T. rex bellowed again, melting enough snow so that now its relatively tiny arms were free to claw at the air. At this rate, in no time those very same arms would be free to claw at anything and everything, including Mr. Cheeseman and his children.

"Hurry!" Chip instructed.

"Quit yelling at me," said Penny through half-frozen lips. "I'm trying, but he's too heavy." Penny's feet slipped out from under her and she folded to the ground. Chip, left to bear the full weight of his father, also slipped, and the three of them now lay in a crumpled mess at the bottom of the hill. Chip stood up and brushed the snow from his jeans. A few tears of frustration escaped Penny's eyes as she cradled her father's head, keeping it off the frozen ground. She could feel herself begin to crack under the stress of this terrible situation.

"Would you please shut up?" she pleaded with the T. rex. "Leave us alone!"

Ignoring Penny's plea, it roared again, melting yet more snow with its fiery exhaust. Pinky barked furiously, though in this instance, the Cheeseman clan certainly didn't need a psychic dog to tell them that danger was looming, as it was looming so ridiculously close to them and with such absurdly wild teeth. Another blast of hot air shot out from the beast's angry mouth, and the tops of its legs were now visible.

"Okay, change of plans," said Chip, not knowing exactly what change he intended to implement. He stood for a moment, trying to think of what his father might do in this situation. He looked up the hill, then back at the winter wonderland spread out across the valley floor, covered with snow and populated with frosted pine trees. "We're going that way."

Penny seemed perplexed by the very idea of such a thing. "But the professor said that if we don't get Dad out of the cold . . ."

"I heard what the professor said," Chip retorted. "But it's going to take us at least a half hour to get Dad up that hill, if we can do it at all. And in another ten minutes that thing is going to be free from the snow and hot on our trail again."

Penny was not one to back down when she felt she was right. "What difference does it make if he eats us when we're halfway up the hill or halfway across the valley? At least if we go up, we've a chance to save Dad's life."

"I hate to be the voice of doom and gloom," said the professor, who actually very much enjoyed being the voice of doom and gloom. "But it seems there's no place we can go to be safe from those teeth."

"I know a place," said Teddy.

"I'm sure you do," said Chip. "But for right now, could you please be quiet? We're trying to think here."

"But there is one place can go where he won't be able to eat us," insisted Teddy, who, like his sister, was not willing to be bossed around when their very lives were at stake.

Chip exhaled sharply and glared at his younger brother. "He's thirty feet tall. Even if we could get to those trees over there and manage to climb up one of them, he'd eat us right off the branches like corn on the cob. Now listen up, everybody. We've got to put our heads together and try to think of something . . ."

Without warning, Teddy took a running start and leaped onto Chip's back, wrapping his arms around his brother's neck.

"Hey!" Chip called out. "What do you think you're doing? This is no time for clowning around."

"Bite me," said Teddy.

"That's crass," snapped Penny. "Now get down from there."

"I'm serious," Teddy insisted. "Try to bite me."

Chip thought for a moment and realized that, indeed, Teddy was not being crass, but quite literal. He turned his head side to side as far as it would go each way. "No way," he said.

Teddy dropped to the ground. "Why not?"

"You want us to climb onto the back of a Tyrannosaurus rex? Are you crazy? What do we do after that? Stay there until he gets so old that his teeth fall out?"

"No," said Teddy. "You just stay there long enough to blindfold him."

"Blindfold him?" said Professor Boxley. "Interesting."

"Isn't it?" Teddy agreed.

"He can't bite us if he can't see us," said Gravy-Face Roy.

"I hate to say it," said Penny, "but it kind of sort of makes a little bit of sense. I think."

Chip looked back at the T. rex, then up at the steep hill, then out across the valley, then down at his father, stretched out on the snow, unconscious. "Okay," he said finally. "We'll give it a shot."

The next thing to do was to try to find something that could be fashioned into a blindfold big enough for an animal roughly the size of a convenience store. Quickly, Chip shed his jacket. "Okay, everybody. Coats off."

"But I'm cold," Teddy protested.

"I hear it's quite warm inside the esophagus of a T. rex," said Penny as she and the professor each removed their jackets and handed them to Chip.

Teddy relented and slipped off his jacket. "I wish I had two sock puppets," he muttered while hopping in place and blowing hot air into his bare right fist. "One for each hand."

Chip's frostbitten fingers made the job difficult, but he managed to tie the four jackets together at the sleeves. That was the easy part. The T. rex was becoming more ambulant with each passing second and with each burst of hot air it spat out. Climbing onto its back and remaining there long enough to complete the job would be the hard part. Chip circled around behind the T. rex, took a deep breath, and hoped it would not be one of his last.

"Be careful," said Penny. Chip said nothing, but turned to Penny with an incredulous look. Penny shrugged. "What? I'm just saying."

Chip managed a brief smile, realizing that his sister was only voicing her concern for his safety. And, with that, he proceeded to do something he never in his life thought he'd find himself doing. He climbed up the scaly backside of a hungry dinosaur and reminded himself that this was one battle he would have to win.

ADVICE ON WINNING

Always remember: quitters never win—but if both sides quit, it's a tie.

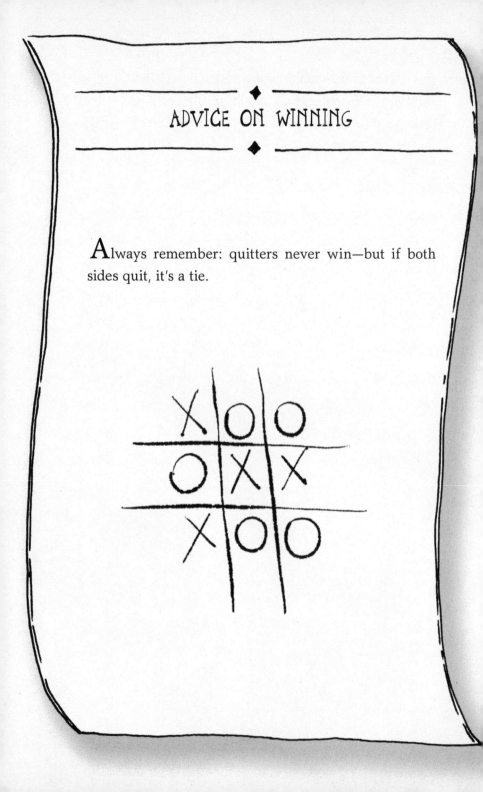

CHAPTER 4

Take a moment to imagine how utterly boring a rodeo would be if bulls enjoyed being ridden by men in funny hats with sharp things on their boots. It's likely that few would pay for the privilege of watching a perfectly contented bull saunter around with a grown man on its back. I imagine it would be every bit as exciting as watching someone pushing a shopping cart. Depending on where you buy your groceries, it is highly unlikely that you will ever see anyone pushing a shopping cart while yelling "Yee haw!" regardless of how good the sale on paper towels might be.

However, the point is moot, because the fact is that no untamed animal will tolerate having a person sitting on its back. This includes bulls, horses, whales, Chihuahuas, and extinct animals such as the Tyrannosaurus rex upon which Chip was currently climbing.

The dinosaur's enormous head swung side to side as it tried in vain to sink its snarled, murderous teeth into its uninvited guest. Chip fought to stay aboard its back. Were he to fall, it could mean a very quick end to him and the others. Chip's hands trembled with cold and fear as the T. rex let go with another nerve-racking bellow, melting more snow and making it even more mobile than before.

Chip's first attempt at slinging the homemade blindfold across the eyes of the great lizard met with futility, as did his second and third. Each time he let go with one hand, the scaly ogre nearly tossed him to the ground, and he was forced to abandon his efforts in order to focus on staying alive.

"Come on, Chip. You can do it," Teddy cheered.

"You're the man," Gravy-Face Roy chimed in.

Penny was too nervous to cheer and instead just dug her teeth into her bottom lip and held her breath. Professor Boxley tugged anxiously on his mustache, so hard that before he realized it he had pulled out a good portion of the right half by the roots, leaving an odd-looking bald spot on his upper lip. If something happened to Chip, how would he explain to Ethan, his friend and former student, that he had let his son engage in such a dangerous scheme? He should have volunteered for the mission, but didn't for one simple reason: he was scared to death.

Chip was breathing heavily, his face red with exertion and fear. Once more he swung the jackets up over the dinosaur's face, and this time he managed to catch the other end of them. All that was left to do was to tie a knot around the writhing giant's head, rendering the beast sufficiently sightless. Chip had learned to tie many different types of knots while sailing aboard a stolen pirate ship back in 1668, but there wasn't time for anything fancy just now. A simple granny knot would have to suffice. Fighting against the violent gyrations of the T. rex as well as the numbness in his fingers, he doubled the knot for some added insurance, then quickly slid down the dinosaur's back, landing silently in the powdery snow.

Teddy and Gravy-Face Roy let loose with a wild cheer while Chip took a moment to evaluate his efforts. He was pleased to see that the T. rex now looked perfectly ready for a game of bite the tail off the donkey. The coats sat across its eyes like a pair of sunglasses made of a cotton/polyester blend. If it looked silly before, with its regrettable orthodontia, the T. rex was now downright comical. But this was no laughing matter, especially to the hopping mad dinosaur.

"Okay," said Chip. "Let's get out of here while we still can." He raced over to his father and, with Penny's help, lifted Ethan beneath his arms. "You two take his feet," he said to Teddy and the professor.

No sooner had they taken Mr. Cheeseman by his feet than the T. rex was finally able to pull its own feet from the snow. It stepped forward, and everyone froze. Not literally, though they were quite cold. They froze in one place, afraid that the slightest sound might alert the hungry carnivore to their precise location. The T. rex took another step forward, and another, until it was ambling blindly into the valley.

"I told you it would work," whispered Teddy. "He can't see us."

The jackets may have blinded the T. rex and angered it, but they didn't stop it from running, full speed ahead, right into a pine tree. Teddy could not help but snicker at the sight of snow from the tree pouring down onto the dinosaur's oversized head. "Shhh," Penny admonished. But it was too late. The dinosaur heard the snicker. It turned, took off running, and promptly collided with a second pine tree. This time they all fought back giggles. Though they may have been flirting with frostbite and hypothermia, there was still something quite funny about watching a blindfolded, buck-toothed Tyrannosaurus rex repeatedly plowing face-first into a series of trees.

Like an eight-thousand-pound pinball, it continued to smack into the helpless pines, bouncing off one and into another as it stumbled its way across the valley floor. Chip and the others resisted the urge to let out a cheer as the dinosaur soon disappeared into the trees and the thick winter mist. A celebration would have been premature. If they hoped to survive, they would first have to get back up the hill to summer.

Chip and Penny walked backward, shuffling slowly up the slick slope while Teddy and the professor waddled after them. Their progress was painstakingly slow. Though Ethan was still very much alive, the fact that he was unconscious officially qualified him as dead weight. Without their jackets to help shield them from the icy wind, their body temperatures continued to dip with each difficult step they took.

It is important to remember that when undue strain is placed regularly upon a muscle, that muscle will gradually grow bigger and stronger in order to accommodate the additional burden. It is also important to remember that the heart is a muscle. For the past two years since the death of their mother, the Cheeseman children had carried with them an incredible emotional weight. Now, what their arms and legs lacked in strength, their mighty hearts more than made up for.

After nearly forty minutes of struggling against gravity, without so much as the strength to look over his shoulder, Chip asked Teddy, "Are we getting close?" Teddy lifted his heavy head and managed a tiny smile. The top of the hill was but steps away. Though the smile was weak, it gave Chip and Penny the extra strength they needed to drag their father up and over the edge of the slope.

But when they were finally able to set Ethan down, it wasn't on the sun-warmed grass of mid-July. It was on hard, cold snow. To their horror, disappointment, and utter confusion, winter had swept in and taken over the entire plateau that just an hour before had been home to perfect weather. Sometimes, when too much strain is placed upon a muscle, that muscle, including the heart, can break.

"No," said Chip, sinking to his knees. "It can't be."

The others just stared out at the endless stretch of snow that covered the ground as far and as wide as the eye could see. Pinky let out a whimper and thought how nice it would be to have a full coat of fur like a normal dog.

The cold wind swirled around them, carrying off precious body heat. The sun seemed as if it were a gazillion miles away, when it was actually only ninety-three million miles away, which is still a very great distance. To give you an idea as to just how far that is, if you were to take ninety-three million miles and lay them end to end, they would reach all the way to the sun. That's a long chunk of space, and now the sun seemed farther away than ever.

"I'm cold," said Teddy. "I want to go inside."

"There is no inside," said Chip. He was physically and emotionally spent, and for the first time in his life, he felt himself giving up. "There's just outside right now, Teddy. Lots and lots of outside."

"I don't understand it," said Penny. Her tears froze half-way down her crimson cheeks. "Why is this happening to us? We broke the curse, so why are all these terrible things still happening to us?"

Chip had no answer for Penny, because there was no answer. The curse of the White Gold Chalice was a vile hex on par with Montezuma's Revenge, but without all that dashing off to the bathroom. It was beset upon the family when their great-great-great-great-great-grandfather, Gentleman Jibby Lodbrok, stole the Chalice back in the 1600s. But when the Cheesemans traveled back to 1668 and returned the chalice to the Duke of Jutland, the curse should have been broken, and perhaps it had been. It was entirely possible that this latest streak of bad luck had nothing to do with the curse, and everything to do with the fact that time travel is still a highly unpredictable and unreliable business.

"What are we going to do?" asked Teddy.

"Who cares?" said Penny. "What's the point of anything? Even if we survive, we're stuck here in Some Times. We'll never get back to save Mom."

"Penny, please," said Chip. "We have to try to stay calm and figure out what to do. How about you, Professor? Do you have any ideas?"

"No," the professor murmured. He hung his head, ashamed that a man of science such as he had no clue what to do. "I'm afraid not."

Chip closed his eyes and could feel himself losing the battle against pessimism. "Then I guess we wait here and hope that the weather changes again before we all freeze to death."

And that's just what they did. They sat on the frigid ground, hopeless and jacketless, huddled together in a single, shivering cluster, waiting for the return of summer or the departure of all feeling in their frozen limbs, whichever came first.

CHAPTER 5

Experts say that freezing to death is actually one of the more pleasant ways to go, and can result in a feeling of euphoria. Still, given the option, I believe that most people in search of a euphoric sensation would choose a roller coaster over death by exposure.

But the Cheesemans and Professor Boxley were given no such choice as they sat on the harsh, cold ground, their body temperatures dropping quickly and steadily along with any hope for survival.

Hallucinations are common in cases of hypothermia, and Penny was the first to slip into the world of the surreal when she imagined she heard a dog barking. The distant sound was accompanied by what sounded like the buzz of a motor.

"D-d-do you hear th-th-that?" asked Teddy. His teeth chattered so badly he was now chewing his gum involuntarily. "It s-s-sounds like a d-d-d-dog b-b-b-barking."

Though she had no training in psychology, Penny knew

one thing. If two people are experiencing the same hallucination at once, it's most likely not a hallucination at all.

The barking and the humming grew louder, and soon, out from the gloom came one of the strangest sights any of them had ever seen. It was a dog pulling some kind of a sled. On that sled was a man dressed head to toe in animal skins. A wiry yellow beard covered the lower half of his face. He could easily have been mistaken for some type of prehistoric human, but for a couple of key factors.

First of all, he was wearing sunglasses, and scientists are generally in agreement that even the hippest of cavemen did not wear sunglasses, because they had not yet been invented. Secondly, the man's dog appeared to have no legs, and instead made its way across the snowy ground on tracks similar to those you'd find on a bulldozer. And though the dog barked incessantly, its mouth failed to include the appropriate opening and closing that one generally expects to accompany such noises.

"Am I seeing what I think I'm seeing?" asked Professor Boxley with what little strength he had left.

"If you're seeing a robot dog pulling a sled with a caveman wearing sunglasses, then yes," said Penny.

They watched as the sled approached, and hoped its rider and his mechanical dog were friendly. One thing that gave them a certain measure of comfort was that Pinky did not growl, but that might have been because she lacked the strength for it, or because, by now, those muscles she used for growling had completely frozen up. Still, it mattered little. If the man on the sled proved hostile, there wasn't much they could do about it now in their badly weakened condition.

The sled glided up next to the shivering group and came to a stop as the dog continued to emit electronic barking noises through its closed mouth. The well-bundled man stepped off the sled and, from the pocket of his patched-together fur coat, pulled at a small device, about the size of a cell phone. He pointed the gadget at the dog and pushed a button. Immediately the barking noises ceased, and the man returned the remote control to his pocket.

"Please, you've got to help us," Penny pleaded, hoping the man spoke English. "Our father is badly hurt." The man took a moment to survey the situation. Penny could see, in the reflection of his sunglasses, a small, pathetic image of her tightly bunched group. How could the stranger not take pity on such a woeful lot?

The man bent down and took Penny by the left hand and, a little too roughly, pushed her sleeve back, then turned her arm and inspected the underside of her wrist. One by one, he did the same with the rest of them, carefully scrutinizing their left wrists. Once he had finished, he turned and walked back to the sled. Penny and the others sat and hoped he would not abandon them. They watched as he lifted a stack of animal pelts from the back of the sled, then returned to where they sat and dropped the skins in a heap. He peeled off the top one and draped it across Teddy's shoulders, then knelt down and lifted the shivering boy from the icy ground.

While the man carried Teddy back to the sled, Chip took a skin from the pile and covered his father. He passed the next two to Penny and Professor Boxley, then wrapped the remaining one around himself.

The pelts were cold and stiff from exposure to the elements and their effectiveness was not immediately felt, though no one was complaining at this point. It was just nice to have something between the icy wind and their bare, goose-bumped arms. Penny picked up Pinky and wedged the hairless pink dog beneath her arm.

The sled driver returned and helped the others to their feet. Silently, he looked the group up and down, then nodded to Chip, apparently deciding he looked the fittest and ablest of the ravaged bunch. Chip took his father by the feet while the modern-day caveman took him beneath the arms. Together they carried Ethan past the motionless robot dog to the back of the sled.

Next, he climbed aboard the sled, removed the remote control from his pocket, and took aim. The mechanical half dog–half tractor began barking once more as it lurched forward, grinding and yipping its way across the frozen landscape.

The sled was just large enough to accommodate one driver and two passengers, and it seemed to have been unofficially decided that those two passengers would be Teddy and his unconscious father. The others would have to walk. But where were they walking? Penny, for one, wanted to know.

"Excuse me. Where are we going?" She couldn't be sure

if the complete lack of response was due to the man being unable to hear over the howling wind and the barking dog, because he didn't speak English, or because he had simply chosen to ignore the question.

Either way, she didn't ask again, and she and the others hunched their shoulders and bowed their heads against the biting wind and trudged along behind the sled. So utterly exhausted were they that none of them noticed the strange dull light streaking across the heavens, barely visible among the dark, winter clouds. Then again, perhaps they had seen it, but thought nothing of it in a place where the moon, the stars, and the sun all hung in the sky at once.

They slogged along for what seemed like an hour (but in reality was only fifty-seven minutes) before they finally arrived at the opening to a cave. The man shut down the electronic dog and stepped off the sled.

The man motioned to Chip, and the two of them lugged Ethan into the cave with the others following close behind, still not quite certain whether their host was friendly or perhaps desirous of putting them into some kind of home-made caveman stew.

Once inside, the first thing they noticed was just how gloriously warm the cave was, though not so warm that they considered shedding their furry blankets. What they next observed was just how little this cave resembled a prehistoric home. Hanging across the length of the far wall was a string of lights, the kind you might expect to find on a Christmas tree or a backyard patio.

In the middle of the dirt floor was a fire pit, and spaced

evenly around the pit were four leather chairs that looked as though they had been pulled from an automobile. Adorning the walls were cave drawings, the type often seen in a history book, except that these paintings were not dull and faded. They appeared freshly made, the colors strikingly brilliant. Among them were a scene depicting a herd of antelope; another of a group of people gathered in a circle, presumably dancing; and one crudely drawn image of a man on a sled being pulled by a mechanical dog.

Chip and the stranger gently lowered Ethan to the floor next to the pit, where a fire was in its last stages but still gave off plenty of heat from the glowing embers that remained. The man motioned to the chairs and said, "Grab a seat."

"You can talk," said Chip.

The man seemed amused by this. "Of course I can talk," he said.

Penny sunk into one of the bucket seats and tucked her knees up to her chin. Chip, Teddy, and the professor took the three remaining chairs. Teddy leaned forward and held his hands above the fire pit. He found the sensation surprisingly unpleasant; the warming of his hands was accompanied by a dull ache as the flesh slowly came back to life.

"Well," said Chip, "it's just that you hadn't said anything up until now."

The man removed his sunglasses. Beneath them his eyes were dark, and held a look of mischief, malice, or both. Chip could not decide. "I like to think before I speak," he said.

"You mean, like, for a whole hour?" Teddy asked.

The man said nothing, but did appear to be thinking as he shed his hat and coat, revealing a slim frame tucked into modern clothes: well-worn jeans and a dark blue polo shirt. His hair was a wild mess of blond curls. "If that's what it takes to get it right, dude," he said.

"Dude?" said Chip, more to himself than anyone else.

"Thank you for saving us," said Penny. "But as you can see, our father's been badly injured. Is there a hospital nearby?"

"And try not to think about it too long," chirped Gravy-Face Roy. The snide remark earned him a flick on the head from Penny, who was growing ever more weary of having to apologize for her little brother and his ill-mannered sock puppet.

"Sorry about that. My brother has a habit of never thinking before he speaks. Unlike yourself, Mister . . ."

"Jones," the man said. "Name's . . . John Jones."

John Jones? Is that the best he could do? thought Chip. Whoever this guy was, he could use some lessons in coming up with fake names.

Using their own phony names, Penny and the others introduced themselves to the so-called Mr. Jones, and did so quickly, as they were anxious to get back to more important things. "The hospital," Penny said. "Is there one close by?"

"Nearest one's in London," said Jones. "Usually about ten miles from here."

"Usually?" said the professor. Such a statement only

made sense in the context of Some Times, where things seemed to change at a moment's notice.

"Yeah; once in a while it's a little farther. But certainly no more than fifteen miles. Twenty-five tops. If it's more than thirty, I'd be surprised."

It was quickly becoming apparent that accuracy was not one of Mr. Jones's strong suits.

"But it's, like, early 1500s London," he continued. "Sometimes mid-1500s, so that's probably not your best bet. Could end up with, like, a face full of leeches. Next closest hospital's in Baltimore in the 1970s, so the prices are pretty good. Either way, I wouldn't recommend taking him back into the cold right away."

"Do you expect it to clear up soon?" asked Chip.

"Yes," said Penny. "What does the weather report say?"

This made Jones laugh. "Weather report? So my assumption was right. You're outsiders." No sooner had he said the words than Jones appeared to second-guess the wisdom of having done so.

"Outsiders?" Chip repeated. "What makes you think that?"

For a moment, Jones said nothing, apparently deciding whether to answer or ignore the question. Finally, he said, "I can tell you're outsiders because when I found you, you were, like, totally lost and confused. To the locals, everything here in Some Times makes perfect sense. But to the outsider, it's an absolute mess."

Things were getting stranger by the minute, Chip

thought. If he and his family were the first to discover Some Times, how did Jones know its proper name? It would be like Columbus showing up in the New World and having the natives greet him with a hearty, "Hey, Chris, welcome to the West Indies."

"You're an outsider too. Aren't you?" said Chip. Jones bit the inside of his lip and narrowed his eyes, but said nothing. Tired of waiting for a response, Chip persisted. "Where are you from?"

"Well," said Jones, "you certainly are a curious bunch, LOL."

Penny looked at Chip and Chip looked at Penny. No question, this Jones fellow was a bit of a strange bird, but did he really just say what they thought he said?

"Excuse me," said Penny. "But did you say LOL?"

"Yeah, you know, LOL," said Jones. "As in, *ha ha ha.*"

"Or *laugh out loud,*" said Chip.

"Oh yeah," said Jones. "I suppose it could mean that too. It's just a way of, like, saving time where I come from."

"How much time are you really saving by saying LOL instead of laugh out loud?" asked Penny. "Or, if something really is funny, why don't you just laugh out loud and not say anything?"

Jones shrugged and said, "IDK."

"You mean *I don't know?*" asked Chip.

"Exactly. Just another time saver."

"We have them where we come from too," said Penny. "But we only use them when typing or texting, not when speaking."

Jones crinkled his forehead and looked thoughtful once again. "I'm sorry," he said. "But what's typing again?"

Chip wasn't quite sure whether a man with a mechanical dog could seriously not know what typing was. He pantomimed the act for Jones's benefit. "You know, it's what you do on a laptop computer."

"Oh," said Jones, as if suddenly remembering some obscure fact from a history exam taken long ago. "We don't have laptop computers where I come from. We have eyetops."

"You replaced computers with basketball shoes?" said Teddy.

"He said *eyetop*, I believe," said Penny. "Not *high-top*."

"What the heck is an eyetop?" asked Gravy-Face Roy.

As Jones went on to explain to Professor Boxley, the three Cheeseman children, and a sock, an eyetop was a computer about the size of a contact lens that fit right over the cornea of the eye and was operated not by typing, but simply by thinking. If his story was true, it meant one thing for certain: wherever Jones came from, it was a world far more advanced than their own.

"Are you from the future or something?" Teddy asked.

"I guess you could say that," said Jones.

"I knew it," said Teddy, who was over the moon at having been right twice in one day.

"But I'm also from the past," Jones continued, taking a little wind out of Teddy's sails. "With time, everything is relative. We're all from the past and we're all from the future, depending on the point of reference." Before Jones could expound upon the topic, two dark creatures scurried into the cave. Teddy sprang to his feet.

"Look out!" he shouted. "Gorillas!"

It was true that the two beings appeared somewhat gorilla-like. Their posture was similar, and their hairlines plunged so low on their sloped foreheads that they threatened to eclipse their eyebrows. Though it was difficult to be certain through all that facial hair, one of the creatures appeared to be male, the other female.

Penny was aghast at what she saw, a scene right out of the museum of natural history. "Those aren't gorillas. They're Neanderthals."

"That's right," said Jones, rising to his feet. He nodded toward the more female looking of the two and said, "Allow me to introduce my wife, Gurda. And that dude over there is my brother-in-law, Stig." Stig emitted a low grunt and a bob of his fuzzy head.

"Stig?" said Teddy, with a sneer that wrinkled his nose.

"Yes," said Jones. "It's a very common caveman name." (See? Told you.)

Jones turned to the furry hominids and spoke to them in a series of staccato grunts and sweeping hand gestures. They responded with a few grunts of their own, and seemed to be talking about the unexpected guests in their cave. Jones answered them by launching into what looked to be a rather elaborate game of charades. He appeared to be reenacting his encounter with the Cheesemans and their subsequent journey back to the cave. As he spoke, the two

Neanderthals wandered over and began inspecting their visitors, sniffing and gently prodding them.

Gurda took a handful of Penny's auburn hair and studied it intently. Penny stiffened, afraid to move.

"Don't worry," said Jones. "She's just being friendly."

Gurda grunted out something that sounded to Penny like an angry growl.

"She says she likes your hair," said Jones.

"Oh," said Penny. "How do you say *thank you* in Neanderthal?"

Jones said something that sounded like *arg schnerr*, but when Penny tried to repeat the phrase, it didn't come out quite the same and resulted in a look of vast confusion from Gurda.

"You just asked for more minestrone soup," said Jones.

"There's a Neanderthal word for *minestrone soup*?" said Chip.

"Well, of course," said Jones, as if that were the most absurd question in the entire history of question asking.

Penny looked up at Gurda and forced a smile. "I don't really want minestrone soup," she said.

"I do," said Teddy. "I'm starving."

"Me too," said Gravy-Face Roy.

Gurda smiled at Teddy and the others and seemed satisfied that there was nothing to fear from the strangers in her home. With a few final grunts, she and Stig waddled to the far end of the cave, where they promptly began smashing several large roots by placing them on a big, flat rock that seemed to serve as the kitchen table and striking them repeatedly with smaller rocks.

"Isn't she something?" Jones said with the smile of a man in love. "Great sense of humor too. And the world's best cook, IMO."

"In your opinion?" said Penny.

"Well, I'll let you judge for yourselves. She makes this casserole that's, like, out of this world. Do you guys like roots and berries?"

"Roots?" said Teddy, who, more and more, was beginning to think that *out of this world* would be a good place to be.

"They're very good for you," said Jones. "Lots of fiber."

"So . . . you married a Neanderthal?" asked Penny.

"Well, we totally fell in love, so, like, why not?" said Jones, a little defensively. "I believe you should be able to marry whomever you choose, don't you?"

"Well, yes," Penny agreed, though secretly she thought that Jones and Gurda were probably the strangest pairing she'd seen since the time that Pinky, a fox terrier bred for fox hunting, developed a severe crush on Digs, a little brown fox from the seventeenth century.

Chip thought they made a rather bizarre couple too. In fact, there were a lot of strange things about this John Jones character, if that really was his last name, and Chip greatly doubted that it was. Whatever his name, Chip had a million questions for him, but they would have to wait, because the Cheesemans were about to get the first good news they'd had all day. It came when Ethan, for the first time since being buried under a mountain of snow, opened his eyes.

"Look!" Teddy exclaimed. "It's Dad. He's awake!"

Chip and Penny rose quickly from their chairs and knelt at their father's side.

"Dad, are you okay?" Penny asked.

From his position flat on his back, Ethan stared up at his young inquisitor and narrowed his eyes in thought. "What is going on here?" he said.

Chip turned to Penny to find his sister wearing the exact same look as his own. It was a look of confusion, and what caused that look was not what Mr. Cheeseman had said, but how he had said it; in a very distinct and very thick Italian accent.

Ethan sat up and took in his surroundings with an arched eyebrow. If the eyes truly are the windows to the soul, anyone looking at Ethan's eyes would quickly determine that he was not at home and that he now had a houseguest. "Would someone be so kind as to tell me where I am? And while we're at it, who are you people?"

"Why is Dad talking like that guy from the pizza commercial?" Teddy asked his older siblings.

"I don't know," said Chip. "Dad? What's wrong? Don't you recognize us?"

Ethan looked at Chip with bemusement, then said, in a rather indignant tone, "Young man, you obviously have me confused with someone else. My name is Rossini. Gioachino Rossini."

"Oh no," said Penny. "He thinks he's Rossini."

"He thinks he's pasta?" exclaimed Gravy-Face Roy.

"What? That's rotini," said Penny, never stopping to

consider she was using precious oxygen for the purpose of correcting a gravy-stained sock. "Rossini was one of the greatest composers of classical music who ever lived."

"Was?" shouted Ethan, waving his hands in the air. "I will have you know I am currently working on my most important opera yet. It will be the masterpiece by which all others are measured."

At first, they wondered if this was their father's idea of a prank, even though he was not one to engage in practical jokes, simply because, as a scientist, he found them to be entirely impractical.

Ethan's head suddenly jerked to one side and his eyes shot up and over as if he were straining to listen to a sound very far away. He began softly humming a tune, slowly increasing its volume, until soon his hands were slicing through the air like an orchestra conductor.

"Hey, I know that song!" Teddy exclaimed. "It's the Lone Ranger."

"Actually, it's called the *William Tell Overture*," whispered Professor Boxley, who happened to be a connoisseur of classical music.

"Hmm," said Gravy-Face Roy. "That sure is a weird name for a song about the Lone Ranger."

Abruptly as he began, Ethan stopped, then stood up and exclaimed, "Quick! I must have a fountain pen and paper at once!" Though none of them knew just what to make of Ethan's strange new persona, it seemed to be unofficially agreed upon that, for the time being at least, they would go with it.

Penny looked to Jones, who seemed thoroughly confused by the entire situation. "Do you have a pen and paper?" she asked.

"I have some paper, but no pen. I'm sure Stig wouldn't mind if you used some of his cave paints."

"Paint?" Mr. Cheeseman spouted. "I cannot compose with paint!"

"Hmm." Jones thought further. "I'd loan him my eyetop, but I haven't used it in so long I totally forgot the password."

"Why do you need a password for a computer that's attached to your eyeball?" asked Teddy.

"Well, in case someone steals my eye, of course," said Jones, as if this made perfect sense. "Don't you have crime where you come from?"

"Not the kind where people steal your eyeballs," said Gravy-Face Roy.

"I have a pencil," said Professor Boxley. He removed the stubby writing instrument from his pocket and found that the point had not survived the avalanche. Luckily, he also had a small plastic sharpener.

He handed the items to Ethan, and Jones sent Teddy to get the paper, which was sitting on a small metal shelf across the room. Teddy retrieved it, but not without a very dramatic huff. It was bad enough to be bossed around by your own family, but to be ordered about by complete strangers was something else. He returned with the paper and handed it to the person whom he had known his entire life as his father, but was now forced to refer to as Signor Gioachino Rossini.

"Grazie," said Ethan in perfect Italian. Up to that point, his knowledge of the language had been limited to words like *spaghetti, pepperoni,* and *mama mia.*

"Let's get you set up at the kitchen table, Signor Rossini," said Jones to Mr. Cheeseman. "I'm sure Gurda won't mind if you do a little composing while she smashes roots." Jones spoke to Gurda in that guttural caveman language. Gurda returned a few grunts and Jones smiled. "See?" he said to the others. "I told you she had a great sense of humor, LOL."

Once Mr. Cheeseman, a.k.a. Signor Rossini, had taken his position at the table and had begun composing his latest opera, Chip, Penny, and the professor gathered around the fire pit to discuss the situation with Jones. Meanwhile, Teddy, sick and tired of being bossed around, wandered throughout the cave, with Pinky on his heels, snuffing and snorting at each and every corner. Teddy found the underground home much larger than it appeared at first glance.

In two years on the run, Teddy and his family had stayed in some pretty interesting houses. There was the old white farmhouse with the creepy attic. There was the little house that smelled like damp wood, which was odd for a house made of brick. And who could forget that house with the flat roof that had been painted the color of pea soup? It featured burnt-orange carpeting throughout, which Penny and Teddy would pretend was molten lava, forcing them to make their way through the house by jumping from one piece of furniture to the next.

But of all the houses they'd been in, this one was the strangest. There were several passages throughout the cave leading to several different rooms, all of them illuminated by the same type of tiny lights that hung across the wall of the main room.

Some of the rooms were empty. One was heavily stocked with food and other supplies. Another appeared to be a bedroom, the floor covered with animal skins and woven blankets. A room much smaller than the rest, located near the very back, contained nothing but a small, cardboard box. Teddy could not resist. Quietly, he inched into the room, toward the mysterious container. Pinky gave the box a curious sniff, then Teddy's curious fingers reached out slowly and pulled back the tattered flap. Cautiously, he leaned over and peered inside the box, then nearly fainted at what he saw.

ADVICE FOR AN ENJOYABLE NIGHT AT THE OPERA

Last weekend, I went to the opera, because I am a sophisticated and refined person of impeccable taste, and because I won two free tickets in a burping contest.

The opera was called *Aida* and was performed entirely in Italian, which, despite recent strides, is still considered a foreign language. In fact, most operas are performed in Italian, so, in order to make your opera-going experience a more enjoyable one, you should first attempt to familiarize yourself with a few simple Italian words and phrases. For instance, *amore* is one word you will hear often, as it is the Italian word for love, or for what happens when the moon hits your eye like a bigga pizza pie.

By brushing up on my Italian before the big show, I was able to surmise that *Aida* is the story of an Ethiopian princess who falls in love with an Egyptian prince and is hit in the eye with some pizza. And, as if that weren't tragic enough, in the end Aida and the prince are killed.

Now, don't go getting the idea that all operas are tragedies and that an evening at the opera has to be a depressing one; many of the great operas are comedies.

It all depends on what you think of someone getting a face full of cheese.

Either way, you'll want to bring along a set of binoculars, known as *opera glasses*, to ensure that you get a ...iew of all that slapstick comedy—or, as it may be, ...k tragedy. And, because ...erage opera can run ...l of four hours, you ... your binoculars to ...f boredom by look-...ugh the wide end ...ending the people sit-...nd you are actually very far away.

"Hello over there!" you shout. "Would anyone like to challenge me to a burping contest?!" And, if you holler loudly enough, security will wrestle you to the ground and see to it that you never go to the opera again. This is not as bad as it sounds, because, as you will soon see, you don't have to actually go to the opera in order for it to one day save your life.

CHAPTER 6

Ethan Cheeseman sat at the stone slab table, scribbling so furiously that his pencil broke every couple of minutes. Luckily, he was very amused by the sharpener Professor Boxley had given him, and so the frequent breakage seemed to have no ill effect on his mood or on his frantic composing. He wrote as if driven by the music in his head, his eyes transfixed on the paper, his hand stopping only to sharpen the pencil or to wipe away a bit of spattered root that landed on the page as the result of Stig and Gurda's equally enthusiastic mashing.

So engrossed was he in his work, he had no idea that only a few feet away, people were talking about him. "I don't understand it," whispered Penny. "My dad doesn't even like classical music. He thinks it's for old people."

"That's right," Chip agreed. "In the car, he makes us listen to classic rock, which we think is for old people."

"And I'm sure he's never even heard of Rossini," said Penny. "So what happened?"

Jones thought for a short time. "Well, I'm no

psychologist, but I'd say it's probably like introjection, IMHO," he said, saving an entire .3 seconds by using an abbreviation for *in my humble opinion.*

"Introjection?" said Penny. This was a word even she, with her absurdly high IQ, had not heard before.

"A theory of Freud's," offered Professor Boxley. "It's the process of absorbing personality traits from an outside source."

"That's right," said Jones. "There are so many imposing historical figures in Some Times that it's possible for outsiders to find themselves taking on a foreign psyche."

"By why this one?" asked Penny. "He's a scientist, not a musician. You would think he'd be more likely to wake up thinking he's Galileo or Sir Isaac Newton."

"I'm afraid I don't have an answer for that," said Jones. "Other than to say that Some Times is one crazy place."

"It sure is," said Penny. "Dinosaurs, Vikings, summer and winter, all happening at once. And how is it that you know so much about it?"

Jones shrugged. "You're right," he said. "I'm an outsider, like you. But I've been here a very long time. Twenty-six winters, forty-two springs, thirty-nine summers, and eighteen autumns, so I've pretty much seen everything. But the main reason I know so much about it is that my great-grandfather discovered it."

This was shocking and discouraging news, especially for Chip. The only good thing about being shipwrecked in Some Times was that, if somehow they were able to make it back, he and his family would go down in history as the first to visit this mysterious world. Now they didn't even have that to hang on to.

"I thought we discovered it," said Chip, unable to hide his disappointment.

"Sorry," said Jones, who did not seem sorry in the least. "But it was definitely my great-grandfather. It's well documented. So what are you guys doing here in Some Times? I know you don't work for Plexiwave."

Penny gasped at the very mention of the weapons manufacturing company responsible for the death of her mother. And it was now apparent why Jones had inspected their arms when he first found them: he was looking for a small tattoo worn on the left wrists of all operatives of the evil corporation. The tattoos typically read *3VAW1X319*, or, when viewed in the mirror, *Plexiwave*.

"You know about Plexiwave?" asked Chip.

Jones scoffed at the absurdity of such a question. "Do I know about the company that's taken over the entire world? Duh."

What? thought Chip. Did he just say that Plexiwave had taken over the entire world? And furthermore, did he just say *duh*? The information hit the Cheeseman children like a sharp punch to the gut.

"Plexiwave killed our mother," said Penny. "And now you say they've taken over the world?"

"Afraid so. Where I come from, they run everything," said Jones. "That's why I originally came here. To hide out. So, tell me then—why are you here?"

"We were bounced off the Time Arc on our way back to save our mother's life," said Chip. "And now we're stuck here on account of some stupid dinosaur that decided to smash . . ."

He abruptly stopped talking, because his mouth suddenly stopped receiving instructions from his brain, which was, at the moment, too busy trying to process the information being sent to it by his disbelieving eyes, which were focused on Teddy, standing there, wearing an odd smile. But it wasn't what was on his face that shocked everyone, but rather what was on his hand.

Jones saw it too. He moved toward Teddy, and Teddy stepped back. "What are you doing with that?" Jones demanded. "What are you doing with Steve?"

Sure enough, perched upon Teddy's right hand was an exact replica of the sock puppet his mother had knitted for him before she passed away over two years ago. And, stranger yet, that dead and buried sock puppet named Steve and the one Teddy now held seemed to have the exact same name.

"Steve is mine," Teddy insisted. "My mother made him for me."

"Obviously, you're mistaken," said Jones. "If Steve was yours, then how would he have gotten into my cave here in the middle of Some Times?"

"I don't know," said Teddy. "But he's mine. You can even ask my brother and sister."

He could've asked Chip and Penny, but they were struck

speechless by the sight of a grown man arguing with an eight-year-old boy over ownership of a sock.

"I believe that you think he's yours," said Jones. "But he's obviously mine. Now please take him off. He's very old. Steve was a gift from my grandfather."

As Teddy and Jones continued to squabble over who had exclusive rights to the ratty old sock puppet, something suddenly occurred to Penny.

"Excuse me, Mr. Jones?"

"Huh? Yes, what is it?"

"You say that Steve was a gift from your grandfather. Just out of curiosity, what's your grandfather's name? His real name?"

Jones placed his hands on his hips and pushed out a long, slow breath. He looked at Penny, then, one by one, at the rest of the strangers in his cave. "Well," he said. "I guess I can trust you. My name's not John Jones."

"I didn't think so," said Chip.

"It's Moss. Sullivan Moss." The name meant nothing to Chip and the others, but what Mr. Sullivan Moss said next was truly astonishing. "And my grandfather is the famous author Simon Cheeseman. Perhaps you've heard of him."

Teddy's arms dropped limply to his side, causing Steve to slip off and fall to the dirt floor. When he did, Sullivan took the opportunity to scoop him up and place him on his own hand. Teddy didn't so much as bat an eye, for he was, at that moment, in a state of shock. Since he and his family had been forced to go on the run, Teddy had used so many aliases that he had almost forgotten his real name. Hearing it now, for the first time in two years, was weird, to say the least.

"That's *my* name," he whispered. *"I'm* Simon Cheeseman."

"That's an awfully strange coincidence," said Professor Boxley.

"Or is it?" said Penny. Without realizing it, she began pacing like a lawyer on cross-examination. "Your great-grandfather, Mr. Moss, the one who discovered Some Times—was his name Ethan Cheeseman, by any chance?"

"Why, yes," said Sullivan. "He was one of the greatest scientists who ever lived. The reason I became a physicist myself."

Chip smiled, beaming with pride. "Would you like to meet him?" he asked. "He's sitting right over there."

Sullivan looked at Ethan scribbling away and muttering to himself in Italian while Gurda and Stig sat across from him, battering roots into a fine paste. "That's Ethan Cheeseman?" Sullivan's mouth dropped open in amazement.

"Best student I ever had," said Professor Boxley.

"So this means you were right," said Sullivan. "You and your family *did* discover Some Times."

"That's exactly what it means," said Chip.

"Yes," said Penny. "It also means that our little brother is your grandfather." Penny threw her arm across her little brother's shoulders, but the news did not sit well with eight-year-old Simon Cheeseman.

"What?" he gasped. "No, no, no. I'm not a grandpa. No way."

The man they initially knew as Jones and now knew as Sullivan Moss looked at Teddy, previously and once again known as Simon, and a broad smile stretched out across his bearded face. He knelt next to the youngest Cheeseman and hugged him, gingerly, as if he were handling a fragile antique lamp. "Grandpa Cheeseman. I don't believe it."

"I don't believe it either," said Simon.

Then Sullivan took Steve and placed him back on Simon's right hand.

"As much as he means to me," said Sullivan, "I'd like for you to have him, Grandpa."

"No, no," said Simon with a sense of panic. He pulled away from Sullivan's clutches. He was much too young to be someone's grandfather, particularly someone who was a good fifty years older than him. "This isn't happening. This is horrible."

"Didn't you hear what he said, Simon?" asked Penny. "He said you're a famous author."

Suddenly, the situation didn't seem so awful, even though Simon had never entertained the idea of becoming a professional writer. His dream job had always been official product tester at a factory that makes inflatable bouncy castles, or to be the guy who rides on the back of the garbage truck. But famous author didn't sound half-bad either. Simon said the words out loud to see how they sounded all strung together. He even added a few extras for effect. "World famous, award-winning author Simon Bartholomew Cheeseman."

"It's got a nice ring to it," said Gravy-Face Roy.

"Who asked you?" said Steve. It seemed the two sock puppets had gotten off on the wrong foot, so to speak.

As the rival socks continued to bicker, it seemed that Pinky was no fonder of this Steve than she had been of the original, and she displayed her lack of affection for the puppet by snarling each time he spoke in his trademark squeaky voice, which sounded not unlike a squealing hamster running on a wheel that was in desperate need of oil.

Sullivan interrupted all the quarreling, snarling, and squeaking by launching into a series of stories about his grandfather. It was as if he'd been waiting years to tell them and could barely speak fast enough to get them out. He told the one about the time they went to the fair together and got cotton candy. Then there was the time Simon took him to the carnival and they got cotton candy. In fact, most of the stories involved cotton candy in one way or another.

"How about me?" asked Chip, both excited and apprehensive at the thought of knowing what his future held in store. "What happens to me?"

"If you're my grandpa Cheeseman's older brother, you must be my great-uncle, Jason," said Sullivan.

Hearing his real name for the first time since this whole ordeal began had a liberating effect on fourteen-year-old Jason Cheeseman. Though changing names every few weeks had made being on the run slightly more bearable, it felt nice now just to be himself again. "That's my name," he said with a smile. "So, what happens to me? Go ahead, I can take it."

"I can't tell you," said Sullivan.

"You can't tell me?" Suddenly Jason was awash with dread. Why couldn't his great-nephew tell him about his future? What had happened that was so horrible that he refused to share it?

"Well, I suppose I could tell you," said Sullivan with a wink. "But I'd rather show you. Come on."

Sullivan led the way, and the others followed him down the long, stone hallway to the tiny room at the very back. He walked to the lonely box sitting in the middle of the room, then bent over and reached inside. "This is my box of keepsakes and good luck charms and stuff," he said.

"That's where I found Steve," said Simon.

Sullivan pulled something from the box, turned, and threw it to Jason, who snatched it out of the air with one hand. Jason looked at the baseball and, when he turned it over in his palm, smiled at what he saw. It wasn't just a baseball; it was an *autographed* baseball, and it had been autographed by none other than Jason Cheeseman.

"So, does this mean . . . ?"

"It totally does," said Sullivan. "It means you're one of only two players to have ever thrown a no-hitter in the World Series."

"Wow." Chip could scarcely contain his excitement. Just knowing he was destined to fulfill his lifelong ambition made him feel as if he could fly.

"You can keep that," said Sullivan. "It'll inspire you during tough times."

Jason rolled the ball over and over in his right hand,

practicing the special grip for each of the pitches his father had taught him to throw using scientific principles.

"What about me?" asked Penny. "What about my future?"

Sullivan smiled warmly at Penny. "My great-aunt Catherine," he said. He placed his hand on her shoulder, and his face adopted a look of immense pride and respect. "And when I say *great*, I mean that in more ways than one. After all, how else would you describe the first woman president of the United States of America?"

From the box, Sullivan retrieved a small, circular pin, bearing the words *Cheeseman for President*. He pinned the campaign button to Catherine's shirt.

"Seriously? Me? The first woman president?" Young Catherine Cheeseman's mind raced with visuals of her meeting with world leaders, delivering inspirational speeches, and making decisions that would affect hundreds of millions of people. She imagined what it might be like to have her image on the new thousand-dollar bill or on a commemorative stamp.

"Yup," said Sullivan. "First and last." Sullivan's demeanor had suddenly darkened.

"What do you mean, *last*?" said Catherine.

"I mean," said Sullivan, "that there will never be another president of the United States of America, man or woman, because it's now the United States of Plexiwave."

Jason gripped the ball tightly and grit his teeth. "We've got to try to stop them from taking over. But without the LVR-ZX, we're stuck here. How do we get back?"

"I don't know," said Catherine. "But we will get back. It has to be that way, don't you see? The fact that you're now holding that baseball means that we made it back. And, more importantly, the fact that Steve exists means that Mom lived to knit it for Simon. It means that we must have found a way to save her life. Somehow we were able to get back!"

CHAPTER 7

A light, quiet snow fell upon the rooftop of a small house, sitting in a small town, located in a big world, situated somewhere along the ever-expanding Time Arc.

Inside, Christmas music played through the dozens of speakers Ethan had rigged up around the cozy home. Also heard was the voice of Olivia Cheeseman, speaking in a tone she reserved for those rare occasions when one of her children had done something to displease her.

"Simon Cheeseman," she said.

Simon was in his bedroom, busy organizing his collection of dirt clods shaped like celebrities, when he heard the call for front and center. He decided it best to leave the clumps of dirt for now and hurry off to the living room to avoid making whatever trouble he was in any worse.

He found his mother standing in front of the mantel, her lips pursed and her hands upon her hips.

"Listen, mister," said Olivia, with no idea that she was speaking to a future famous novelist. "How many times have I told you the nativity scene is not a toy?"

Sure enough, his six-year-old brain had failed to remind him to remove the evidence, which consisted of a half-dozen green plastic army men standing atop the stable and a toy dinosaur positioned next to the three wise men. Wedged between the dinosaur's mighty teeth was a sheep.

"Sorry," said Simon.

"Don't be sorry," said Olivia. "Just don't do it, okay?"

She snatched the dinosaur and the other nativity interlopers and handed them to Simon. "Now go get your boots and your coat. We're going to get the tree."

As Simon hurried off to the closet, his mother assured him that he had not ruined Christmas after all. She did this by reaching out and giving his spiky blond hair a good scruffing up.

While Simon fetched his coat and boots, Jason and Catherine were busy in the kitchen, stringing popcorn and cranberries, which was a good way to decorate a tree inexpensively. It was also a good way to start an argument.

"No, no," said ten-year-old Catherine. "You're doing it wrong."

Jason looked down at his handiwork resting on the kitchen table and saw nothing but popcorn-and-cranberry-stringing perfection. "What do you mean?"

"You're putting four popcorn, two cranberries, three popcorn, and two cranberries."

"Yes," Jason agreed. "And?"

"You're supposed to be putting four popcorn, two cranberries, three popcorn, and *one* cranberry."

"What's it matter?" asked Jason, thinking his little sister

must be joking. To Jason it may not have mattered at all, but to the owner of a superorganized, highly scientific brain like Catherine's, it mattered very much.

"Symmetry," she said. "If we don't use the exact same pattern, the tree will lack symmetry."

"Ahh," said Jason. "I finally get it now. The true meaning of Christmas is symmetry."

"You're mocking me," said Catherine. "I don't enjoy being mocked."

The argument could go no further, because Olivia stuck her head in and said, "Get ready, you guys. We're going to get the tree."

"I hope we get a symmetrical one," said Jason, happy to get in one last dig.

In the garage, Ethan stood amid a shower of sparks as he welded together two sheets of metal that would form part of the outer shell of his Luminal Velocity Regulator. When he finally lowered his torch and pushed back his welder's mask, he saw Olivia standing in the doorway to the house.

"I'm getting close," he said with a smile. "A couple more hours and I should have the entire fuselage ready to assemble."

"Yes," said Olivia. "Too bad it'll have to wait."

"Wait?" said Ethan. "For what? This is perhaps the greatest invention in the history of mankind, and it's just about finished. What could be more important than that?"

"We're going to get a Christmas tree, remember?" Being married to a brilliant scientist for the last fifteen years, Olivia had become used to Ethan forgetting important dates and engagements, including, but not limited to, her birthday, his birthday, their anniversary, soccer games, baseball games, Valentine's Day, St. Patrick's Day, the Fourth of July, the Fifth of July, Easter, and Christmas.

"Oh," said Ethan. "Well, couldn't you guys just go without me?"

"It's not as if we're going to the supermarket to pick up milk and bread," said Olivia sternly. "We're going to get a Christmas tree. All of us. Together. Now."

Ethan smiled. He loved his wife for many reasons, one of them being that she always put her family above all else. "Right," said Ethan. "I'll get my coat."

It could be fairly stated that, as a whole, the Cheesemans were generally a happy bunch; but around Christmastime, they were all the more joyous, and their holiday cheer was palpable as they piled into the family station wagon and buckled up.

Pinky, looking very festive in her bright red Santa hat, which matched her reddish brown hair very well, climbed up onto Olivia's lap and settled in for her annual ride to the Christmas tree lot.

"Okay, everybody ready?" asked Mr. Cheeseman.

"No," said Catherine. "We need some music."

"Right," Mr. Cheeseman agreed. He flipped on the radio, and the beat-up station wagon, its occupants singing "Jingle Bells" at the top of their lungs with unintentional harmony and some intentionally incorrect lyrics, pulled out of the driveway of the little white house as the snow continued to meander slowly from sky to ground. So full of holiday cheer were the Cheesemans that they took no notice whatsoever of a long black car parked just down the street, its tinted windows concealing the nastiest of villains with the hollowest of cheeks.

So bony was Mr. 5's sweaty face and so sunken were his eyes that he looked like a skeleton with a coat of paint. "Look at those idiots," he said to his evil cohorts. Positioned behind the wheel was the enormous Mr. 88, the ringed fingers of his meaty left hand tapping the steering wheel. In the backseat were two men dressed like the others, in black suits and ties. They were Mr. 207 and Mr. 70, who was filling in for Mr. 29, who was out that day with a bad head cold. "All these fools throwing away good money on worthless Christmas trees. The whole thing is a waste of time and money."

"That reminds me," said Mr. 88 with a smile. "I'm taking my nephew to the mall to see Santa Claus this weekend."

"You don't have to say Santa *Claus*, you know," said Mr. 207. "You could have saved time by just calling him *Santa*. We all know who you mean."

"Well, I could have been talking about Santa Barbara."

"Who's Santa Barbara?" asked Mr. 207.

"I think that's one of his helpers," said Mr. 70.

"Would you all just shut up already?" fumed Mr. 5, his bony hands clutching at the air in front of him as if choking an imaginary throat. "Santa Barbara is a place, not a person!"

"Well, it must have been a person at one time," said Mr. 207.

"He's got a point," said Mr. 88. "They wouldn't name a place after a fake person."

"What about Indiana?" asked Mr. 70.

"What are you talking about?" sneered Mr. 5.

"You know, Indiana Jones. He's a fake guy, and they named a whole state after him."

Mr. 5 looked as though his bald, skeletal head might spontaneously combust at any moment from the pressure building up from within. "How do you people manage to dress yourselves in the morning? Now listen, we're here for one reason and one reason only. We've got a very important job to do. Is that something you imbeciles can get through your thick skulls?"

The three imbeciles nodded their thick skulls and mumbled the start of an apology before trailing off.

"Okay, let's move," said Mr. 5.

The four Plexiwave employees exited the car and walked toward the Cheeseman house, the falling snow covering their tracks as they went.

"One thing I don't get," said Mr. 207. "Why does Santa Claus have a Spanish first name and a German last name?"

"Good question," answered Mr. 88. "And why is he also called Saint Nicholas?"

"Maybe Santa Claus is short for Saint Nicholas," offered Mr. 70.

"What?" scoffed Mr. 207. "How the heck is Santa Claus short for Saint Nicholas?"

"You know," said Mr. 70. "If you say Saint Nicholas really fast, it kind of sounds like Santa Claus."

Both Mr. 88 and Mr. 207 gave it a try and found Mr. 70's theory to be entirely plausible. "You're right," said Mr. 88. "It *does* sound like Santa Claus if you say it really fast." He said it seven or eight more times in a row before Mr. 5 stopped in his tracks, spun around, and glared at Mr. 88.

"All right, that's enough!" Mr. 5 moved his face so close that Mr. 88 hoped he did not intend to use a lot of words that began with the letter *P*. "I've had it with you pinheads and all your preposterous poppycock! I don't want to hear one more word about Santa Claus or Saint Nicholas or Father Christmas or anybody else like that. Have I made myself perfectly clear?"

The men shuffled their feet and gave a nod and a single-shoulder shrug. Mr. 88 wiped the spit from his forehead.

"Good," Mr. 5 continued. "Now, Mr. 88 and I are going to enter through the back door and do what we came here to do. And while we're engaged in our very important work, you two nimrods are going to stand watch. Any questions?"

"Uh, yes," said Mr. 70. "What about Kris Kringle?"

DECORATING TIPS FOR THE HOLIDAYS

Christmas is a time for gathering with family and friends to celebrate, reminisce, and sing songs about the malodorous nature of Batman. It is also a time to spruce up the house by going out and getting what Germans call a *tannenbaum*, what vegetarians call part of a balanced breakfast, and what the rest of us call a Christmas tree.

Most people, including the Cheesemans, get their annual tree from a commercial Christmas tree lot. To get the full experience, however, I believe you need to go out and chop down your own tree. Sure, it's a little more work, though I must say it helps if you live, as I do, close to a good-sized city park.

Once you've gotten the tree home and you're certain you were not followed, you should set the proper mood for the decorating experience. Start by putting on some seasonal music and gathering up some wood for a big fire. Now, unless you live out in the country, the wood-gathering part may prove to be a challenge. Perhaps you've noticed that your neighbors rarely use their doghouse or porch swing.

Now that the fire is blazing and the house is at a toasty womb temperature, you may commence with the decorating. First, take your tree and place its trunk in the customized stand, which, with its three opposable thumbscrews, looks like some type of evil torture device designed to force Christmas trees into giving up valuable information.

"All right, Tannenbaum, who sent you? Who do you work for?"

"Ahhhh! I don't know what you're talking about! I'm just here to provide a little Christmas joy for a couple of weeks, then dry up and get tossed into the gutter! That's all, I swear it!"

Now, with the tree firmly fixed in its upright position, it is time to cover it with popcorn, cranberries, and other things your dog will enjoy eating when you're not home. Assuming you have a dog.

And, if you do, I advise you to leave it at home for protection when going out to buy the tree. Otherwise, villains may seize the opportunity to break into your house for the most evil of purposes.

CHAPTER 8

The longest journey begins with a single step. I'm not sure who first said that, but odds are it was someone who did not own a car.

Either way, the crux of the matter is that in order to travel anywhere, you must first have a means of getting there. With the once-football-shaped LVR-ZX now as flat as Kansas, the Cheesemans seemed to have no way of getting to where they wanted and desperately needed to go.

"There is one way," said Sullivan, thoughtfully stroking his ratty yellow beard. "The LVR-ZX may be destroyed, but there's still the LVR-TS714 version 8.0."

"What the heck is an LVR-T . . . 4 . . . something-something?" asked Simon.

"It's a time machine," said Sullivan. "How do you think I got here, by astral projection? LOL."

LOL indeed. Suddenly it sounded as if getting to where they wanted to go was going to be a piece of cake. All they had to do was hop into Sullivan's time machine, hit a few buttons, and they'd be there in no time. There was only one problem.

"Where is this time machine of yours?" asked Jason.

"Don't worry," said Sullivan. "It's well hidden. And I think I remember where."

"You *think* you remember?" said Catherine.

"Pretty sure," said Sullivan. "I bet we'll be able to find it. Of course, it doesn't have any seats. Or lights, so it won't be the most comfortable ride. But other than that, it should be good to go."

No sooner had Sullivan spoken these words than Signor Rossini slammed his pencil onto the table and rose up from the bucket seat that had once belonged to the LVR-TS714 version 8.0. "I must get to a piano immediately!" he shouted while waving his latest composition in the air.

Gurda grunted something, and Stig and Sullivan each snorted out a laugh. Apparently Gurda *did* have a very good sense of humor.

"Yes, Mr. Rossini," said Catherine. "We'll get you to a piano right away." She hoped, as did the others, that once they managed to get Ethan out of Some Times and back to the real world, he would snap out of whatever this spell was that he was under. "Mr. Moss, how soon can we leave?"

"Please, call me Sullivan. Or Sully. I can't have my great-aunt and the future former president of the United States calling me *mister.*"

Catherine smiled. "Okay, Sully. How soon can we leave?"

Sullivan said nothing, but walked to the entrance of the

cave and looked out. Apparently he did not see his shadow, because, when he returned to the group, he announced that winter was over and it was now summer, with a slight chance of spring later in the day. "We can leave right away," he said.

"But there are dinosaurs out there," said Professor Boxley, not wanting to sound like a coward, but also not wanting to suffer the indignity of wetting his pants again. "And Vikings and Huns and who knows what else."

"We don't really have much of a choice, I'm afraid," said Jason. "Either we take the risk and try to find this hidden time machine, or we all stay here for the rest of our lives, living in a cave and eating roots and berries."

By now it was beginning to get somewhat darker than it had been. Though day and night seemed to be coexisting, the light remained sufficient for traveling and, presumably, for finding hidden time machines.

It was decided that they would take the sled and the mechanical dog along to make the journey easier and to carry any supplies they might need. These included a few tools should the LVR-TS714 version 8.0 be in need of any repairs, being that it had been sitting in its secret hiding place for the past twenty-six winters, forty-two springs, thirty-nine summers, and eighteen autumns.

As Sullivan pointed out, the runners of the sled could be removed and replaced with wheels, which would do better on the bare ground now that the snow had melted away and the earth had begun to bake in the hot summer sun of late evening.

"That's a pretty awesome dog," said Simon.

"Thanks," said Sullivan. "His name is Rufus. You can pet him if you want. He doesn't bite, unless I push the right button. I made him from stuff I took off the LVR-TS714 version 8.0."

Simon gave Rufus a tentative pet.

"Wait a minute," said Catherine sternly. "You stripped the time machine? Our only way out of here?"

"I took only nonessential parts," said Sullivan. "You know, like chairs, lights, cup holders. Stuff like that. Like I said, it won't be a comfortable ride, but it should still get you where you want to go." He smiled and gave a hearty double thumbs-up, which did little to instill confidence.

"I don't understand," said Jason. "Why would you strip parts from the time machine? Even if we hadn't come along, you'd still need it to get back yourself."

"Oh, I have no intention of going back," said Sullivan. "I'm a married man now. I couldn't leave Gurda. And I couldn't bring her back with me. They'd put her in a museum."

"Or on a reality show," said Catherine.

"LOL," said Sullivan, which sadly indicated to the others that, in the future, there were still reality shows. He then attempted to lift the sled and flip it over, but couldn't manage it. "Whew, that's heavy," he sighed. "Would you mind giving me a hand, Uncle Jason?"

"Can we help too?" asked Simon, referring to himself as well as to Steve, who occupied his right hand, and Gravy-Face Roy, who sat upon his left.

"Sure, Grandpa. I'll take all the help I can get."

Jason and Catherine snickered at this. "Please don't call me *Grandpa*," Simon implored.

"Well, what should I call you?" asked Sullivan.

"How about *Gramps*?" suggested Catherine.

"Or maybe *old-timer*," Jason offered.

This was normally where their father would have intervened and put a stop to the teasing, but, of course, Ethan was no longer with them, and Signor Rossini was off on his own, slicing his arms through the air and humming the tune in his badly bruised head. They were all anxious to have their dad back, but none so much as Simon.

"Okay, on three," said Sullivan. They all took hold of the sled and tried rolling it over. As they struggled with the task, Gurda seemed to appear out of nowhere to provide that extra bit of muscle necessary to turn it belly-up.

Without a word, she returned to the cave, and Sullivan watched her with admiration. "You can see why I fell in love with her."

"You do seem very happy together," said Catherine. "Where did you meet, anyway?"

"At a discotheque in the 1970s," said Sullivan. "Would you hand me that wrench, Grandpa?"

With a huff, Simon grabbed the screwdriver with his Gravy-Face-Roy-covered hand and passed it to Sullivan. Not only was he the lone eight-year-old grandfather in existence, he was now being bossed around by his middle-aged grandson. Unbelievable.

"Wait a minute," said Jason. "You mean you met your Neanderthal wife at a discotheque from the 1970s?"

"Yeah, you should see her do the robot," Sullivan boasted.

"You met your Neanderthal wife at a discotheque from the 1970s and danced the robot," Catherine confirmed.

"Yeah. Isn't Some Times amazing? Everything happening at once. I mean, where else could you go skiing in the morning, then spend the afternoon at the beach, lying in the sun and looking at the stars?"

"Or get eaten by a T. rex with buckteeth," said Professor Boxley, his eyes darting nervously back and forth.

Sullivan laughed. "Oh, you mean Trixie. I've had a couple of run-ins with the old girl myself." Sullivan removed the runners from the sled and replaced them with wheels stolen from some nonessential parts of his LVR-TS714 version 8.0.

"It does seem awfully dangerous here," said Catherine, looking around at the wild and barren landscape that surrounded the cave. "Why would anyone choose to live in such a ridiculously hazardous place as Some Times?"

"That's part of the appeal," said Sullivan. "Where I come from, everything is so safe. You know you can't even take a shower without wearing a helmet? It's the law now."

"How do people wash their hair?" asked Catherine, to whom such things were of great importance.

"They don't," said Sullivan. "But it doesn't matter, because you pretty much have to wear a helmet wherever you go, so no one ever sees your hair."

When the sled-turned-wagon was loaded with supplies, Sullivan said good-bye to his lovely wife, Gurda, with a tender kiss and to his brother-in-law, Stig, with a hearty and hairy handshake. They would've come along, Sullivan explained, but Gurda had her hot yoga class and Stig was way behind on his hunting and gathering. And so, Stigless and Gurda-free, they started out on their uncertain journey to find the hidden time machine and, for Signor Rossini, a working piano.

Sullivan fired up Rufus, the robot dog, and Simon, Professor Boxley, and Pinky climbed aboard the wagon while the others walked alongside. They were promised by Sullivan that the LVR-TS714 version 8.0 was absolutely, positively, without a doubt no more than five miles away. Six or seven at the most. And certainly not more than eight.

As they left the safety of the cave behind, Jason could not seem to think about anything other than his recently discovered destiny of pitching a no-hitter in the World Series. He gripped the souvenir ball in his hand, the horsehide smooth in contrast to the roughness of the stitches. He imagined standing on the mound, the crowd of fifty thousand rising to its feet as he went into his windup and delivered a wicked forkleball. The batter swings, and the ball punches the catcher's mitt with a glorious *smack*. Strike three, game over, no-hitter, and Jason is carried off the field and into the record books.

So lost was he in fantasy that he didn't realize he was making fake crowd noise with his breath as he walked.

"What's wrong, Jason?" asked Catherine with a sly grin. "You sound like Darth Vader having an asthma attack."

"Huh? Oh," said Jason. "I was just, uh, thinking about something."

"Baseball?"

"Yeah."

Future President of the United States Catherine Cheeseman had also been thinking about her destiny. She had never seen herself as a politician; at this point in her life, she really wasn't sure what she wanted to do. In school, she had taken a career aptitude test, which involved answering scores of multiple-choice questions by coloring in tiny dots with a number-two pencil. After all of that careful coloring in of all those dots, the results stated that she would be best suited to working in a factory that makes Japanese flags.

"Pretty crazy, isn't it?" she said, admiring the campaign button. "To know what life holds in store for you? Though, to be honest, I'm not sure I want to be president. Too much pressure."

Jason shrugged. "Could also be fun. Maybe I'll arrange it so you can throw out the first ball at the World Series."

"Gee," said Catherine. "Then I'll be sure to have something to put in my memoir."

"Maybe you can get Simon to write your memoir for you."

"Good point."

As they walked and talked, something suddenly occurred to Jason. If his great-nephew was middle-aged, that meant that in Sullivan's world, Jason would be dead, which bothered him greatly at first. Still, did he really want to be alive in a time when helmets were required in the shower and the world was run by the evil Plexiwave empire? Then again, if he and his family had anything to say about it, there was no way Plexiwave would take over the world.

CHAPTER 9

Once upon Some Times, there was a family of time travelers who had found themselves stuck there (in Some Times, that is) while wanting nothing more than to find their way out of that dreadful place. As they set off to find the machine that very well might make that possible, they found that the terrain in Some Times was as unpredictable as the weather. One minute the ground was hard and flat, the next hilly and covered in deep, shifting sand that made walking slow and arduous. They traveled through an overgrown meadow, then into a grove of gnarled oak trees, then out onto a stretch of dry, cracked earth.

Sullivan suddenly removed the remote control from the wagon's cup holder and used it to stop Rufus in his tracks. The rest of the group stopped as well and watched as Sullivan took a moment to chew a bit on the inside of his lip and pull worriedly at his beard.

"Sullivan?" asked Catherine.

"Of course we're not lost," came Sullivan's preemptive response. "It's just that things look a little different this time, that's all. I'm absolutely, positively, one hundred percent sure it's this way. Easily ninety percent, that's for sure. Seventy-five percent at the very least. I think we've got at least a fifty-fifty chance of finding it if we keep going this way."

"I am losing patience," grumbled Ethan in broken English. "I must have access to a piano." For emphasis, he waved his composition in the air before folding the pages and shoving them into his pocket.

"Don't worry, Signor Rossini," said Catherine. "We should be at the opera house soon."

"We had better be," he said with a scowl. "Otherwise I will find it on my own."

As Jason and Catherine exchanged a look of concern for their father and wondered if he would ever return to normal, Sullivan started Rufus on his uncertain journey once again. Another half hour had passed when they began to hear some type of commotion. It grew louder as they drew nearer to the source.

Just up ahead, not more than a quarter mile, there were hundreds, perhaps thousands of busy people, engaged in various tasks, moving like ants across the desert floor. They were building something, and as the wagon neared, it became apparent just what that something was.

"Wow," gasped Catherine. "They're building a pyramid."

"Well, that's progress, I guess," said Sullivan.

"I can't wait until it's finished," said Simon.

"Well, you're going to have to wait, Grandpa Cheese-man," said Catherine. "Looks like they've got a few years to go."

The structure appeared to be about one-third finished, and, as with any large construction project, some people were working while others only pretended to work, and some made no attempt to look busy and just stood around, talking. Though Catherine found the scene nothing short of fascinating, Pinky did not like the situation one bit and signified so with her trademark warning of danger.

"Maybe we should ask those guys for directions," said Simon.

"That's a dumb idea," said Gravy-Face Roy.

"I think it's a great idea," said Steve.

"Yeah," said Catherine. "Great idea. Let's all learn to speak Egyptian, then we can wander down there and ask them if they would be so kind as to direct us to the nearest abandoned time machine."

"That was sarcastic, wasn't it?" asked Simon.

"You're catching on," said Catherine.

After a quick discussion, it was officially agreed upon that they would not ask the ancient Egyptians for directions, and would instead continue to rely on Sullivan's sketchy recollection of where he had stashed the time machine. And so, they gave the ancient construction site a wide berth as they passed, barely drawing notice from the workers, the talkers, or the guys pretending to work.

By and by, they crested a small hill, and Sullivan stopped

and scanned the landscape, left to right. "Wait a minute," he said with a bob of his head. "I think we're getting close now. Yes, I believe I hid it in an abandoned mine just over there to the left. Hundred percent sure. Eighty percent at the very least."

The electronically yapping dog lurched forward and made a sharp left turn. They followed the wagon down the hill, where they saw yet another construction site, this one far less ancient than the first, as evidenced by the fact that it seemed to be the future home not of a brand-new ancient pyramid, but of a brand-new shopping mall. There were bulldozers, a towering orange crane, and, as with the previous site, some people working, people pretending to work, and others just standing around talking.

"Uh-oh," said Sullivan, because he could think of nothing better to say. He was a hundred percent certain, eighty at the very least, that this is where he had chosen to store his time machine for safekeeping all those winters, summers, and springs ago. Now the abandoned mine was home to a sprawling shopping complex, which, when finished, would feature no fewer than three coffee shops and a place that sold deep-fried cheese.

Jason and Catherine stood and stared and hoped that Sullivan had made a mistake, something he certainly seemed capable of doing. Professor Boxley nervously bit his nails.

"Are you sure?" Jason asked. "Are you sure this is the place?"

"IDK," Sullivan responded.

Ethan scoffed in Italian and spat out a puff of Italian-sounding air. "This is the most hideous opera house I have ever seen. It's no wonder they're tearing it down."

"Uh . . . yes," said Catherine. "But don't worry. I hear the new one is going to be spectacular."

Without another word, Sullivan drove nearer to the site, and the others followed. They approached the enormous crane, which would have been quite helpful in the building of a pyramid. Sullivan continued on, and just beyond the crane he and everyone else stopped in their tracks.

Rusted, dented, and dust-covered, the LVR-TS714 version 8.0 sat on the gravel-strewn ground, looking like something completely incapable of traveling along the Time Arc.

"Is that it?" asked Jason. "Is that your time machine?"

Sullivan shook his head disbelievingly. "I don't know what to say."

"Say it's not your time machine," said Steve.

"I'm afraid I can't do that, Steve," said Sullivan. He stepped off the wagon and his feet crunched through the gravel as he walked toward the badly damaged machine he had built from the ground up with his bare hands. He gazed upon his once splendid creation with extreme sadness. Slowly and gently, he reached out to touch its dusty surface, when suddenly the hatch door flung open.

Out from the egg-shaped time machine walked a man in a fluorescent orange vest and a bright yellow hard hat. And some other stuff, too, of course, like pants and a shirt. And work boots, which ground into the gravel as he stepped from the LVR-TS714 version 8.0.

"You have to jiggle the handle," the man said to Sullivan. "And watch out for the squirrels. They'll bite if you're not careful." He said nothing else, and walked over to the crane and climbed up into the driver's seat. Sullivan was devastated. Not only had his beautiful work of scientific art been rendered completely useless for the purpose of time travel, it was now being employed as a construction site port-a-potty and a home for wayward squirrels.

Sullivan peered inside, confirming what he feared he might find. Besides the obvious accompanying odors, the control panel had been completely torn out, the wires gnawed and frayed by sharp rodent teeth. The LVR-TS714 version 8.0 was a complete and utter disaster.

"Well?" asked Professor Boxley. "How bad is it?"

"I can't believe it," said Sullivan, his voice weak and defeated. "Everything is broken except for the restroom."

"That's horrible," said Catherine.

"That's awful," Jason agreed.

"That's great," said Simon. "Because I really have to go."

"Do you think it can it be repaired?" asked Professor Boxley, looking even more nervous than usual.

Sullivan turned and slumped to a seated position in the open doorway of the time machine. He rested his head in his hands. "Well," he said. "Nothing's impossible. Except that."

"What are you saying?" Catherine demanded. Ever since discovering that Sullivan was her great-nephew, and that she would one day be president, she found herself speaking to him differently, as if she were the adult and he the child. In some ways, that was certainly true.

"I'm saying," said Sullivan, "that it would be faster to build a new time machine from scratch than to try to repair this one."

"And how long would that take?" asked Jason.

"Mom once made a cake from scratch," said Simon. "And that only took a couple of hours."

"We're not talking about a cake here," snipped Catherine. "We're talking about a time machine. And I thought you had to use the bathroom."

"Oh yeah." Simon slipped past Sullivan and into the hollow shell of the time machine, where he would, for the first time in his life, contemplate the wisdom of having a sock puppet on each hand.

"Even if we could find all the parts to build a new one," said Sullivan, "it took me almost two years, working around the clock, to finish this one."

"We can't afford to stay here that long," said Jason.

"Well," said Catherine. "It took one brilliant scientist two years to build this one. We have three of the brightest scientific minds of all time."

"Three?" said Jason. "But Dad's . . ."

"Yes, I'm aware of the situation," said Catherine. Right then and there she decided that she'd had just about enough of the craziness that was Some Times, and she no longer felt like putting up with it. She marched over to her father, took him firmly by the shoulders, and looked directly into his eyes, just as she had seen her mother do on those occasions when Olivia had decided her husband needed a healthy dose of tough love.

"Listen, Dad," she said. "I know you're in there somewhere. And we need you. Mom needs you. So please try. Try to remember. Your name is Ethan Cheeseman. You're a scientist. You're not a composer. Do you understand me? You're not a composer."

With each true statement that sprang forth from Catherine's lips, Ethan's face underwent a gradual change, until finally he sighed heavily and placed his hands on his hips. "I understand," said Ethan, in a thick Italian accent. "You don't like it. You don't like my new opera."

Not only had Catherine failed to evict Signor Rossini from her father's injured head, she had also managed to hurt his feelings.

"No," said Catherine. "It's a beautiful opera. And when it debuts, we'll be the first in line to see it. And you know who else will be there? Olivia. You remember Olivia, don't you?"

For a brief moment, Catherine thought she saw a glimmer of recognition in her father's eyes, but she couldn't be sure. All she knew for certain was that if they could somehow manage to find all the parts necessary to build a time machine from scratch, they would have only two scientists to work on the device and another to write songs about it.

CHAPTER 10

People say that if life gives you lemons, you should make lemonade. This is why unsolicited advice should be left to the professionals, because if life gives you lemons but doesn't also give you a whole lot of sugar, you're going to end up with some pretty awful-tasting lemonade. You might as well advise people that if life gives them a bag of wet sand they should make a stained glass window.

The point is that sometimes life gives you lemons and nothing else, which is exactly what happened to the Cheesemans, who, at that moment, had no use whatsoever for a semisweet beverage—or a stained glass window, for that matter. As resourceful and resilient as they might have been, this time it seemed pointless to even try to make something good out of this horrible situation.

They were years away from finding a means of returning to their own time, and Signor Rossini was still without a piano.

"I can't believe we're going to be stuck here for two

years," said Jason as the beleaguered bunch trudged back toward Sullivan's cave to regroup.

"That's *if* we can even find the parts we need," said Catherine. "It could be end up being a lot longer than that."

"We'll do our best," said Professor Boxley. "We'll work night and day if we have to." Of course, in Some Times, working night and day was something that could be done at the same time.

Suddenly, Pinky stopped and dug her nails into the ground, growling and refusing to move another inch.

"Uh-oh," said Professor Boxley. He was well aware of Pinky's psychic powers and had seen them at work, first-hand. "What's wrong? Why is she growling? What is it this time?"

"I don't know," said Jason. "But something's got her spooked."

It has been said that dogs can predict things like earth-quakes, tornados, and, in this particular case, enormous, earth-shaking explosions.

The sound was that of a two-megaton bomb, and the ground rocked sufficiently as to knock young Simon and his sock-puppet pals to the ground. The immediate result was that all those who had not fallen over froze in their tracks. They scanned the horizon, all 360 degrees of it, and soon noticed the source of the blast. Directly in front of them, perhaps twenty miles ahead, a thick gray cloud rose from a mountaintop and into the blue/black day/night sky.

"A volcano," said Professor Boxley.

"Wow," said Simon, slowly returning to his feet. "Look at all that smoke."

"That's not smoke," said the professor. "It's ash. Now, I'm no expert in the field of volcanology, but I would venture to say that, considering the direction of the wind, that ash is coming this way. And it looks as though it's coming fast."

"What about lava?" asked Simon, again remembering the pea-green house with the orange carpet.

"It's a definite possibility," said the professor, his lower lip visibly trembling. "Either way, I think we should be going as fast as we can away from it."

"No way," said Sullivan. "I've got to get back to the cave and make sure Gurda's okay. She's got a great sense of humor and she's a wonderful cook, but, to be honest, sometimes she's not too bright. She needs me there."

"Well, if we're going to go directly toward the volcano, we should probably hurry," said Jason. And so, without further discussion, Sullivan set Rufus at full throttle, and the group raced off toward the rapidly darkening sky.

As the ash rose higher into the air, it blocked out more and more light, which made it much easier to see the red, fiery glow spreading out across the landscape. Simon's question had been answered. Yes, there would be lava.

Pinky was growling nonstop at this point, using not her psychic powers, but her senses of sight and smell, which told her all she needed to know about what was up ahead.

"I don't like this," said Professor Boxley. "Walking

toward a volcano does not seem like a smart thing to do, speaking strictly from a scientific standpoint."

"You can stop if you want to," shouted Sullivan over Pinky's growling and Rufus's mechanical barking. "But I'm going to find my wife."

"And we're going with you," replied Jason. "We stick together as a family, no matter what. Isn't that right, Signor Rossini?"

It might have been wishful thinking, but Jason was pretty sure he saw a hint of knowing in his father's eyes. But then, just like that, it faded once again.

In a very short time, what one could see in all their eyes were tears and redness caused by the sulfur in the air and the thick ash, which was quickly making its way toward them.

"Cover your faces," ordered Sullivan. "Trust me, you don't want to breath in this stuff."

Jason looked at his little brother, whose hair was now covered with a thin layer of white ash. No doubt, it made him look somewhat more grandfatherly than he had before.

Not only was the air becoming thicker with ash, it was also getting warmer as they approached the lava field that was, at the same time, rapidly approaching them.

"Look there," said Catherine.

It was their bad posture that gave them away as the two Neanderthals slowly emerged from the falling ash and the heat waves that danced and rippled across the ground. Sullivan jumped off the wagon and ran to his wife and brother-in-law. Though none of the outsiders spoke Neanderthal, it was apparent that Gurda was quite upset. Her eyes were doubly red from crying and from the abrasive particles that filled the air.

Sullivan hurried Gurda and Stig back to the wagon. "Our house," he explained to the others. "It's been completely destroyed. Gurda and Stig were lucky to get out alive." He glanced back in the direction of his cave. In just a few short hours, he had lost both his time machine and his home. Still, he was grateful that his wife was alive and well.

Beyond that, there wasn't much time for feeling anything else. The ash and lava were coming their way, which meant that their way would have to change and change quickly if they were to avoid being suffocated, cooked alive, or both.

Sullivan turned the wagon around and they headed back the way they had come, with no clear destination in mind other than away from the ash and lava-spewing volcano.

"My throat hurts," said Simon.

"Mine too," Steve concurred.

"Quit your complaining," said Gravy-Face Roy, bringing his gravy-stained face a little too close to Steve's for the latter sock puppet's liking.

"I'll complain if I want to," said Steve. "You're not the boss of me."

Everyone has their breaking point, and Catherine had officially reached hers. To be fair, it had taken a lot. For starters, her mother had been killed by evil villains, which resulted in her family being forced to go on the run for two years. Returning the White Gold Chalice had left them shipwrecked in 1668, where they were pursued by the evil Mr. 5, a band of ill-mannered pirates, and an overzealous witch hunter. (Just for the record, there is no such thing as an *under*zealous witch hunter.) Rescued by Professor Boxley, the Cheesemans soon found themselves shipwrecked in Some Times, where, so far, they had been forced to deal with a man-eating dinosaur and a brutal avalanche that resulted in the loss of their father to some strange type of amnesia.

Now, after all this, having to put up with a pair of mismatched socks constantly sniping at each other was simply too much.

"All right, you two," she fumed. "Put a sock in it!" She was too angry and too fed up to recognize the absurdity of telling a sock puppet to put a sock in it. "And you," she continued, turning her attention to her younger brother. "If you can't keep those two bundles of yarn quiet, I will happily unravel them and scatter them in the breeze. Is that understood?"

Simon had been reprimanded by his sister countless times in his eight years, but this was the first time he ever felt afraid of her. Even the Neanderthals looked a bit uneasy. "Yes, it's understood," Simon said meekly.

"Good. Now let's move it."

But when Catherine and the others returned to the business of moving it, one member of the group steadfastly refused to join them. Signor Rossini stood with his arms folded, a look of obstinacy upon his face.

"I have followed you people long enough," he said. "You

promise me a piano, and instead you bring me to Pompeii so that I might be killed by a volcano? From now on, I will go my own way, thank you very much."

As Mr. Cheeseman strode away from the group, for a moment everyone simply stood motionless and wordless, communicating with one another by way of befuddled looks. Finally, Jason sprinted after his father and stepped into his path.

"You can't go," he said, half pleading and half demanding.

"What do you mean I can't go?" said Signor Rossini. "Who's going to stop me?"

"I'm going to stop you," said Jason. Never before had he defied or challenged his father in such a way. In doing so now, he felt both shame and an odd sense of exhilaration. "You have to stay with us."

"You people are obviously lost, and I am through traipsing all about the countryside with no idea of where we are going."

"I'm not asking you to stay with us," said Jason. A knot was slowly forming in his stomach. "I'm telling you."

Mr. Cheeseman said nothing. He simply brushed Jason aside and continued on his way. Standing up to his father was something new and frightening for young Jason, but it's not as though he had a lot of other options. If he let his father wander off into the crazy world of Some Times, in all likelihood they would never see him again.

When Ethan kept walking, Jason realized there was only one thing to do. He lowered his head and charged.

Unlike another well-known composer (I'm talking to you, Beethoven), Gioachino Rossini had no trouble at all with his hearing and spun around to find a fourteen-year-old boy chugging toward him like a color-blind bull charging a bright red cloth. He did not, however, see this in time to do anything about it, and soon he found himself flat on his back with the ash-heavy air suddenly and completely absent from his lungs.

His eyes bulged from their sockets as he struggled for breath. He looked at the fourteen-year-old boy sitting on his chest and seemed to be asking why he had just thrown him to the ground.

"I'm sorry, Signor Rossini," said Jason. "I'm sorry I tackled you, but I had no choice."

The others gathered around as the ash continued to filter in, slowly working to blot out the sun, the moon, and the stars.

"Signor Rossini," Catherine said, kneeling next to her father. "Are you okay?"

Finally, Ethan sat up and gave his eyes a couple of good blinks before saying, "What's going on? Where am I? And who the heck is Signor Rossini?"

Jason, Catherine, and Simon looked at one another and smiled the biggest smiles they had in quite some time. As for Ethan, he soon found himself tackled anew as his three overjoyed children piled on and welcomed him back with hugs and, in the case of Pinky, licks to the face. All of this sudden attention left the man both thoroughly delighted and utterly confused.

"What?" he asked. "What's going on?"

"You're back," said Catherine. "You're finally back."

"I'm back? Back from where?"

"From crazy land," said Steve, which earned a predictably stern look from Catherine.

"Hey," said Ethan. "It's Steve. But that's impossible. Steve's dead."

"Not this Steve," said Simon. "This is the new Steve that Mom made for me after we went back and saved her life. I got him from Sullivan."

"Who's Sullivan?" Ethan asked.

Simon nodded in Sullivan's direction. "He's my grandson."

"Your grandson?" said Ethan. "You mean . . . he's from the future?"

"Yes and no," said Simon. "We're all from the past and we're all from the future, depending on the point of reference."

"Wow," said Ethan, impressed with his son's level of reasoning. Then he caught sight of Stig and Gurda. "Excuse me," he whispered, "but are those Neanderthals?"

"That's Stig and Gurda," said Jason. "Gurda is Sullivan's wife. She's very nice, and apparently has a great sense of humor."

Now that Ethan had returned to a state of normalcy, Sullivan was anxious to meet the man who had been so influential in his life.

"Great-Grandpa Cheeseman," he said, offering his hand. "It's an honor to meet you, sir."

Ethan rose to his feet and wiped the ash from his right hand onto his jeans. "Thank you," he said.

"No, thank *you*," Sullivan insisted. "It's because of you that I went into the field of time travel. And it's because of you that I ended up here in Some Times. Everything I have, I owe to you."

"You don't have much now that your house has been destroyed," quipped Gravy-Face Roy.

"Are you kidding?" said Sullivan. "I've got my health, a beautiful wife, and a baby on the way."

Upon closer inspection, Gurda did look to be sporting a small bump in the midsection. She appeared at Sullivan's side, wearing a shy, Neanderthal smile. Sullivan draped his arm gently across her shoulders.

"Did you hear that, Simon?" Jason chided. "You're going to be a great-grandfather."

"Congratulations, Sullivan," said Ethan. "Having children is the best thing that you can ever hope to do. Trust me on that one." Ethan punctuated his statement by scruffing up Simon's hair and applying an affectionate squeeze to the back of Jason's neck. Then, something suddenly occurred to him.

"Hey," he said. "Why are you using your real names?"

"We don't have time to explain," explained Catherine. "We'll tell you later. Right now, we've got to stay ahead of that volcano."

Ethan looked back and saw the swell of fiery lava creeping its way across the landscape. While striving to outpace the encroaching flow of oozing molten rock, Ethan's children tried to fill him in on everything else that he'd missed, including the unfortunate news that, in the future, Plexiwave had taken over the entire world. Ethan was shocked, fascinated, and had many questions, but they would go unanswered for now because just then Pinky stopped, lowered her head, and emitted one of her trademark growls, this one more intense than any they had ever heard before.

SOME UNWRITTEN ADVICE ON WRITING

Of the many subjects children are taught in school, the most important are said to be the Three Rs, which are: reading, riting, and rithmetic. As you may have noticed, rspelling did not make the list.

Of these so-called Three Rs, I believe that writing is by far the most challenging. Seriously, when was the last time you heard about someone suffering from mathematician's cramp? Or reader's block?

"I've been staring at the bookshelf for hours and I can't think of anything to read!"

In addition to being the most difficult of the three Rs, it is also, in my expert opinion, the most important. We humans have been writing ever since we first figured out how to scratch images onto a rock. Several gazillion years later, paper was invented by the Chinese as a means of helping to decrease the size of fortune cookies, which, up to that point, were slightly larger than an adult yak.

This is just one of the many reasons that paper beats rock. And though it's true that scissors beat paper, try writing something with a pair of scissors sometime.

Putting words to paper and doing it well beats everything, though I must caution you that it can also lead to a great deal of anguish, particularly if you are writing a story about actual living people, like the one you are reading now.

Because this book is strictly nonfiction, as the author I can only record what has actually happened, regardless of how much I would love to add a character who is part wombat and shoots laser beams from his snout.

And, being that I am strictly bound by the facts, I cannot guarantee a happy ending. Will the Cheesemans get out of Some Times alive, and will they ever have the opportunity to save Olivia's life? The short answer is, I don't know. And the long answer is, I really, really don't know. At all. For real. Seriously. Dude.

So I strongly advise you to stick with me, buckle up, and hope for the best.

CHAPTER 11

I believe it was Will Rogers who once said, "Everyone is ignorant, only on different subjects," which may prompt some of you to say, "Who the heck is Will Rogers?"

To the best of my knowledge, he was a guy who said stuff. And, though what he's saying here is more or less correct, it is my opinion that we should all be striving to avoid wallowing in ignorance, partly because there are so many preferable things in which to wallow; mud, self-pity, butterscotch pudding.

Besides, it is a scientific fact that too much ignorance, just like too much butterscotch pudding, can kill you. Ways to reduce your personal level of ignorance and, thus, increase your intelligence include: reading, considering other viewpoints, and investing in a psychic dog able to warn you when you are in danger of being eaten by a hungry T. rex.

Yes, there she stood, a mere hundred feet away, in all her bucktoothed glory: Trixie, the Tyrannosaurus rex, now missing the blindfold and several of those snarly teeth, which could be found embedded in the trunks of certain pine trees not too far away. Cloaked in a layer of white ash, she looked like a ghost, and Simon thought she might very well be one. Maybe, he thought, she had fallen off a cliff while blindfolded and had now returned from beyond the grave, seeking revenge. Or perhaps she was just seeking lunch, plain and simple. Whatever she was in search of, and for whatever reason, the fact remained that the Cheesemans and their friends had to figure out a way to prevent the ghastly beast from attaining its goal.

"Okay, now *that* I do remember," said Mr. Cheeseman, staring at the familiar prehistoric face. "I'll never forget those teeth as long as I live."

"Which may not be too much longer if we don't think of something fast," said Jason.

"But there's nothing we can do," Professor Boxley said with a quiver. "There's a volcano behind us and a dinosaur in front. We're doomed."

Jason thought that if the professor had been right every time he'd pronounced them doomed, they'd be dead ten times over by now. Still, this situation looked much more hopeless than any of the other predicaments in which they had found themselves, and he feared that this time the professor may have been right.

Gurda grunted several times, which seemed to irritate Sullivan. "Please, Gurda," he said. "This is no time for jokes." Stig offered a few excited grunts of his own, to which Sullivan responded, "Yes, you're right. That's exactly what we'll do."

"What? What will we do?" asked Simon.

"Tell us," said Steve.

"Be patient," said Gravy-Face Roy.

Sullivan said nothing, but simply stepped off the wagon, first making sure it was pointed directly toward the prehistoric dentist's worst nightmare known as Trixie. She snarled, growled, and clawed at the ground, preparing to charge.

"All right," said Sullivan. "I don't know how much time this will buy us, so when I give the word, run like mad."

Sullivan gave the dog an affectionate pat on the head and said, "Okay, boy. You know what to do." He hit the remote control, and Rufus raced toward Trixie. Then Sullivan gave the word and they all ran like mad, except for Gurda and Stig, who ran more like chimpanzees, their arms swinging side to side, their heads bobbing back and forth as they struggled to keep pace with the humans, who were much better suited to running.

The dinosaur's presence forced them to take a diagonal course away from the spreading lava, allowing it to creep up on them more quickly. Also slowing them down was the absence of Rufus, which left Sullivan to pull the large wagon himself.

Let me just say that those who complain about being between a rock and hard place should try being between a sea of bubbling molten rock and a hard-headed Tyrannosaurus rex sometime and see how they like it.

Ethan and the others choked their way across the landscape as Rufus barked his way toward the baffled dinosaur, who was not so completely baffled that she was unable to raise a foot and flatten the mechanical dog with one powerful stomp. Just like that, Rufus, Sullivan's loyal companion, was nothing more than a pile of scrap metal.

Sullivan's plan had bought them time, but only about thirty seconds of it. Deciding, by way of a few quick sniffs, that a mechanical dog was not a culinary delicacy, Trixie tipped her enormous skull forward and gave chase.

Jason led the group with Catherine right behind him, while Sullivan, Professor Boxley, and the two Neanderthals worked to keep up.

Because Jason was ahead of the pack, he was also the first to slam on the brakes and skid to a sudden halt. When the others caught up to him, they soon saw why he had so abruptly stopped running away from the man-eating beast. He stopped because if he had continued, he would have plunged to his death over the side of a cliff. And not just any cliff.

"You've got to be kidding me," said Catherine, throwing her hands in the air. "The Grand Canyon?"

"Wow," said Gravy-Face Roy. "I've always wanted to see the Grand Canyon."

As if being chased by a hungry bucktoothed dinosaur while trying to avoid being swallowed up by a lake of lava weren't enough, they now had to contend with the fact that they were standing at the edge of a rather large hole in the ground—a hole commonly known as the Grand Canyon.

They whirled about on their heels in time to see Trixie lumbering toward them. Her mangled grill seemed to be sporting a smile. It was not a friendly smile, but more the kind you might see on the face of a child seconds before he devours a plate of cookies he's been instructed to stay away from. Her beady eyes moved back and forth as if she were deciding which of them to eat first.

"Dad, what do we do?" Jason said, his gaze alternating between Trixie and the Grand Canyon. (An excellent name for a rock band, incidentally.)

Ethan knew exactly what to do, but he wasn't about to share his plans with anyone because he was certain that if he did, they would only try to stop him. "I love you guys," he said to his kids. "Do whatever you must to stay alive. And if you ever see your mother again, tell her I love her too."

"Dad?" said Jason, fearful of his father's intentions.

Then Ethan worked his face into a grimace of anger and did the inexplicable. He charged toward the hungry dinosaur.

"Nooo!" shouted Catherine, but it was too late. Ethan was just seconds away from a long drop down the food chain, and his horrified children could do nothing but stand and watch.

Trixie widened her jaws in anticipation. Saliva dripping to the ground made a muddy paste of the fallen ash. And then, just as Ethan was about to find himself mixed, blended, and frappéd with that very saliva, Trixie suddenly lifted her head high into the air and let out a horrible wail. This was not the sound of an angry dinosaur; this was the sound of an injured one.

Jason was the first to notice it; an arrow with half its length buried in the beast's left thigh. But it was the other end of the arrow that proved most interesting. The colors and design of the fletching, those feathers attached to the end that help stabilize an arrow's flight, looked very familiar. Then, with a *whoosh* and a *smack*, another very familiar-looking arrow pierced the animal's throat.

"Look," said Simon. "It's Big."

"I know it's big," said Catherine. "Tell me something I don't know."

"No, it's Big. Right over there."

Sure enough, standing just a stone's throw away was Big, the smallish girl who had stolen Jason's heart in the year 1668. Standing next to her was Digs. To Jason, it seemed like a dream. When he left Big behind, he hoped that one day he would be able to travel back in time and see her again. Never in a million years did he expect to see her here in Some Times, and certainly not just hours after saying good-bye.

Everyone watched as Big reloaded the bow and drew it back. A third arrow ripped through the air and into the T. rex's exposed abdomen. Trixie staggered and stumbled, and Ethan hoped that if she was to give in to gravity she would do it somewhere away from him. But she did not fall. Instead, she swayed left, then right, then turned and hobbled away, disappearing behind a curtain of white ash, bellowing the entire way.

The animal that had caused an entire troop of American Colonial soldiers and a large band of marauding Vikings to go running for their lives had been humbled and sent on its way by a fifteen-year-old girl with a homemade bow and a handful of arrows.

Ethan breathed the biggest sigh of relief he had ever breathed before. The adrenaline rush of having been that close to being eaten alive made him dizzy, and he chose to sit down before he fell over. Catherine and Simon rushed to his side. Jason looked at his father, then at Big.

"Go ahead," Ethan said with a smile. "Go ahead."

This was all Jason needed to hear. He sprinted toward Big, and Pinky ran along beside him. He wrapped the girl up in his arms, her braided ponytails taking flight as the blue baseball cap he had given her fell to the dusty ground.

"I was afraid I'd never see you again," said Jason, still not entirely certain that the girl standing before him was real and not just a product of his imagination. After all, how would she have gotten here from where he had left her in the forest outside a small Danish town in 1668? Then again, if he was dreaming, then Pinky must have been having the same dream, for she was busy chasing Digs, the two playfully darting back and forth.

"I was afraid of that as well," said Big with that soft, cautious smile of hers. "It has been so long."

"It sure has," said Jason. "The longest twelve hours of my life."

"Twelve hours?" Big looked utterly confused. "It's been five months and a day since I last saw you."

"That doesn't make sense," said Jason, and it certainly

didn't. Then he remembered exactly where he was and how nothing in Some Times made any sense at all. "I don't understand it, but I'm sure glad you're here. But how? How did you get here?"

Big spelled out the story of how she had hitched a ride aboard Captain Jibby's ship, making the four-week journey from Denmark to New England. With the help of a kind blacksmith named Mr. Lumley, she was able to repair the time machine, still hidden in the woods where Mr. Cheeseman had left it. It took only a week or so to fix the LVR's damaged ceiling panel. The remainder of the four months, she said, was spent learning how to operate the device. Jason already knew that Big was more than just a pretty face, and the fact that she had managed to master in a mere four months something that even the most accomplished scientists might take years to figure out made him all the more impressed.

And though her desire to see Jason again was certainly a major reason for Big wanting to jump into the LVR and speed along the Time Arc, there were other motivating factors as well. Jason should have realized this before choosing to lecture Big on the dangers of time travel. "You could have been killed," he told her.

"The passion for discovery is in my blood, passed down from my father," said Big. "And no amount of reason or logic can quell that desire. You must understand that. With or without you, I had no choice. So I set the controls for the time and place you said you were from and found myself here, in the future, which, I must confess, is not at all what I'd hoped it would be."

"But this isn't the future," said Jason. "This is Some Times. It's a terrible place, and we've got to get out of here."

"Some Times?" said Big. She scooped up the baseball cap with the white letter P for Police Pals and twisted it back onto her head.

"It's hard to explain." Then Jason thought of something that gave him hope for the first time since their arrival in this strange world. "The LVR," he said. "You came here in the LVR. Where is it?"

"Not too far from here," said Big. "It's very near the ship in which you traveled, the LVR-ZX. When I first stepped out of the LVR and saw the condition your ship was in, I feared you might be dead. But then I saw tracks leading away. And I noticed that the tracks were the same as those I followed through the forest the day I first met you. I knew then that I would find you."

Jason smiled at Big, not with love, but with admiration, which is a different and more meaningful kind of smile. To do as she had done, to hop into a machine of which she had limited understanding at best and travel alone along the unpredictable Time Arc, Jason thought that Big must be the bravest person he had ever met.

In no time, the courageous girl found herself surrounded by the rest of the Cheeseman family, who were almost as happy as Jason was to see her again.

"I must say, I'm in complete awe of you, young lady,"

said Professor Boxley. "What you did took a great deal of both brains and courage."

"And that was some awfully nice shooting as well," said Catherine, who knew a thing or two about archery, having taken lessons for several years.

"Thanks, Penny," said Big, unaware that since she had last seen them, the Cheeseman children had begun using their real names. It had to be explained to her why the boy named Chip, of whom she had grown so fond, was now going by the name of Jason.

"It is my hope," said Big, "that once you save your mother's life, you can stop running and that you'll never have to change your names again."

"That's our hope too," said Gravy-Face Roy, formerly known by such names as No-Face Roy and Rat-Face Roy.

Jason introduced his brave young girlfriend to Sullivan. "This is Big," he said. "Or did you already know that?"

Sullivan smiled at Big. "I already knew that. My great-aunt Big," he said, and gave her a hug. "It's great to see you again." If this were not confusing enough for Big, Stig and Gurda approached her and offered their thanks in the form of a series of grunts. Gurda took a moment to admire Big's beaded braids. The girl seemed wary but tolerant of the intrusion, which lasted only until another blast from the faraway volcano reminded them of the urgency of the situation.

"Okay, we'd better move out," said Jason, not quite ready to relinquish the role of leader that he had assumed while his father was unconscious and in an amnesiac state. "Big says the LVR is close by."

With the ground covered in ash, nothing looked at all familiar. Without an experienced tracker like Big, finding the LVR would have been like finding a noodle in a haystack, which is almost as difficult as finding a needle in a haystack, particularly if you're talking about linguini.

"I don't understand it," said Big. "This concept of Some Times. The idea of being able to travel through time is strange enough. But traveling to several times at once is more baffling to me yet."

"I know," said Jason. "And believe me, I can't wait to get the heck out of here."

Jason's sentiments were shared by all but Sullivan, who had no intention of leaving a chaotic world that seemed well suited to his quirky sensibilities. He agreed to accompany them on their quest to find the LVR, but he had no interest in joining them beyond that.

"It's right over this hill," said Big after they'd walked for about thirty minutes. As they neared the top of the hill, the Cheesemans held their collective breath, half expecting to see the LVR smashed like a grape or torn apart by wild animals. But when they finally laid eyes on it, the LVR was perfectly formed, without the slightest trace of wildlife or construction workers needing to go to the bathroom. With a thin white ash coating, it resembled a giant goose egg—the most beautiful giant goose egg in the history of eggs. Or of geese, for that matter. For once, things seemed to be going their way.

CHAPTER 12

Awesome," said Sullivan, with no shortage of wonderment and reverence. "So this is the original LVR." He walked a slow circle around the machine. He wanted to touch it but refrained from doing so, as if it were some ancient, holy relic. Meanwhile, Ethan carefully inspected the repair work done to the ceiling panel.

"Well, I'll tell you one thing," he said. "That Mr. Lumley is an awfully good blacksmith."

"And an awfully good friend," said Big.

"Do you mind if I have a look at the interior?" asked Sullivan.

"Not at all," said Ethan, and he began keying in the password needed to open the pod door from the outside. But when he finished, he found the door remained locked.

"Oh, sorry," said Big. "I forgot. I had to change the sequence."

"You figured out how to change the password?" Ethan marveled.

"Took me three days," she said, punching in the new

numbers. "I changed it to C-H-I-P so I would always remember." She pulled open the hatch, and Sullivan peered inside.

"Go ahead," said Ethan.

Sullivan ducked his head, stepped into the prototype time machine, and let out a chuckle. "So it's true," he said when he saw the seats and the control panel. "You used parts from an old motor home, LOL."

"You work with what you have," said Ethan.

"I know all about that," said Sullivan. "I used parts from an old 2087 model hover-van for my LVR-TS714 version 8.0." As he inspected the rest of the LVR, his eyes widened and a broad smile pushed that scruffy blond beard aside. "I'd love to take just one ride in it. Maybe someday, if you're ever back this way."

Sullivan stepped out of the LVR and took a few more moments to admire it, then said, "Well, I guess this is goodbye." He turned to Simon and put his hand upon his shoulder. "It was great seeing you again, Grandpa."

For once, Simon didn't mind being called Grandpa. In fact, he found that he rather liked it. It made him feel older and, more importantly, grown-up. Slowly, he pulled Steve from his right hand and offered him to Sullivan. "Here," he said. "I can't take your good luck charm."

"But your mother made him for you," said Sullivan.

"It's okay. After we save her life, and after we go for ice cream, I'm going to ask her to make me a brand-new Steve."

As Sullivan took the tattered sock puppet in his hands, tears formed in his eyes, and Simon hoped it wouldn't damage his eyetop computer like the time Simon had ruined a perfectly good laptop by accidentally dousing it with hot chocolate.

"This is the second time you've given this to me," he said. "I'll treasure it for the rest of my life. Thanks, Grandpa Cheeseman." Sullivan then gave his eight-year-old grandfather one last hug before Jason stepped forward and offered his hand.

"It's us who should be thanking you, Sullivan," he said. "Not only did you save our lives, but you gave us all hope for the future." Jason held up the autographed baseball as proof of this.

Sullivan gave Jason's hand a squeeze and a shake, then turned to the future President of the United States, Catherine Cheeseman. "Don't worry," she said. "We'll stop them. Once we save our mother's life, we'll go after Plexiwave."

"I know you'll succeed," said Sullivan. "You've all got what it takes, and I'm proud to call you my ancestors." He walked to the wagon, lifted the pile of animal skins, and handed them to Ethan.

"Take these," he said. "Just in case. You never know."

Ethan wished Sullivan luck and cautioned him to make sure to turn away from the LVR when the engines kicked in. The bright, bluish light was of such intensity that it could be blinding.

As much as the Cheesemans hated good-byes, they were very anxious to say good-bye, *adios, auf Wiedersehen*, and *sayonara* to Some Times and hello to something resembling what they considered a normal existence. As they stepped into the Luminal Velocity Regulator, they felt relief being somewhere familiar. With one final wave to Sullivan, Gurda, and Stig, Ethan shut the hatch door. He and Professor Boxley wasted no time setting up at the controls.

"That knob tends to stick, I find," said Big, the self-taught scientist and time traveler. "Try turning it as you push."

"Thanks, Big," said Mr. Cheeseman, both pleased and amused to find Big's suggestion worked like a charm. "Okay, everyone. Buckle up. It's bound to be a bit of a bumpy start just trying to get back on the Time Arc."

The children did as they were instructed, and Ethan hit the ignition switch, quickly bringing the engines up to full power. When Ethan took note of the various readings on the control panel, he suddenly looked worried.

"What's wrong, Dad?" asked Catherine.

"The battery. It's pretty low. I just hope it'll take us as far as we need to go." As far as they needed to go was the day before Olivia was poisoned. Ethan punched in the necessary coordinates.

"Okay," he said. "Here we go."

But when Ethan flipped the switch, they went exactly nowhere.

"This is a smooth ride," said Simon. "Doesn't even feel like we're moving at all."

"That's because we're not," said Jason. "Dad, what's going on?"

"It looks as though getting out of Some Times and back onto the Time Arc is going to be more difficult than I thought," said Ethan.

"It's the angle of trajectory," said Professor Boxley. "It's got to be changed to account for the Great Sync."

The Great Sync to which the professor was referring was that mysterious and tenuous connector along the ever-expanding Time Arc where the beginning of time meets the end of time. Hitting it at the wrong angle was what caused them to be bumped off the Time Arc and into Some Times to begin with. Now it was the very same issue that seemed to be preventing their return to the Time Arc.

"Yes, but changed to what?" said Ethan. "The numerical possibilities are endless. We could try guessing, but odds are overwhelming that we'd use up our remaining battery power before we figured it out." Ethan sighed and hung his head. "I hate to say it, but I'm afraid we're going to have to face the facts. We may be stuck here for a while longer while we try to figure this out."

This news was deeply troubling to Simon, terribly frustrating to Jason, and incredibly intriguing to Catherine, who stood up and exclaimed, *"Face the facts.* That's it!"

"What's it?" asked Ethan.

"In the middle of the avalanche"—Catherine scrunched up her forehead and closed her eyes in an attempt to help relive the moment—"I saw Mom, and she spoke to me."

"What did she say this time?" asked Simon. "Did she ask about me?"

"No," said Catherine. "Though I'm sure she would have if there'd been time. But it happened so quickly. She just smiled at me and said, 'Face the music, face the facts, back to front and hurry back.'"

"I'm sorry," said Ethan, who, despite Catherine's history of ghostly encounters, was still skeptical of them. "But I don't see how that helps us."

"I don't see either," said Catherine. She plopped back down into her seat and kicked at the air in frustration. Group morale was plummeting, nearing rock bottom, when Catherine again sprang forth from her chair, this time snapping her fingers and pointing at her father.

"Dad," she said. "I know the answer."

"What?" asked Ethan. "What's the answer?"

"It's in your back pocket."

For all Ethan knew, his back pockets were completely empty. But when he inspected them further, he found several pages of paper. "What is this?" he asked as he slowly unfolded the sheets of paper to find them covered in musical notes.

"It's the *William Tell Overture*," said Jason. "You wrote it when you got conked on the head and thought you were that composer guy."

"Yes, but it's more than just the *William Tell Overture*," said Catherine. "I just know it. It's what Mom was talking about."

Ethan gazed at the pages again, then turned his focus back to Catherine. "Are you saying that within these notes lies the formula we need to get back onto the Time Arc?"

"That's exactly what I'm saying."

"Sounds a bit far-fetched, don't you agree?"

"Not to me," said Big, uncharacteristically inserting

herself into the conversation. "When a spirit speaks to you, it would be foolish not to listen."

"I think so too," said Catherine. "And, after all, we've got nothing to lose, right?"

As ridiculous as the idea may have seemed to Ethan's orderly, scientific brain, he had to admit that, yes, they had nothing to lose, and so he agreed to give it a shot. "I'll scan it into the computer's database and have it convert the notes to numbers," he said. "Then we'll see what happens."

And that's just what Ethan did. And while he performed the task, the others waited, silently and nervously. Simon began biting the fingernails of his right hand. When Catherine gave his hand a slap and told him to stop, Gravy-Face Roy started biting Simon's fingernails.

Following the longest fifteen minutes ever, Ethan finally said, "Okay, the information is loaded and ready to go. Keep your fingers crossed, everybody."

"I thought you didn't believe in superstition," said Professor Boxley with a wink.

"I believe in anything that might help get us out of here," said Ethan. Then he hit the switch and . . . nothing. The LVR did not move so much as a tiny inch or a split second. Even Ethan, who had been so doubtful of the plan, could not hide his disappointment. "Sorry, Catherine."

"No," said Catherine. "It's me who should be sorry, for getting everyone's hopes up with such a stupid idea."

"Pardon me," said Big. "The words that your mother spoke to you. Could you repeat them please?"

"Why?" asked Catherine. "What's the point?"

"Please," said Big.

Catherine relented and again recited the cryptic poem. "Face the music, face the facts, back to front and hurry back."

Big thought for a moment, then said, "Back to front. Perhaps she meant that the music should be entered backward, in reverse order."

Catherine remained despondent, though Big's interpretation of the poem seemed to pique Ethan's interest. "It's possible," he said with a light bob of his head.

"Wouldn't hurt to give it a try, anyway," agreed Professor Boxley.

With a few clicks on the computer keyboard, Ethan reversed the order of the numbers he had entered moments earlier. He took a deep breath, then hit the switch. In a flash, heads snapped back and eyes widened as the LVR lurched forward, careening wildly along the Time Arc. Jason and the other passengers gripped their armrests tightly as the time machine picked up speed.

"We did it!" shouted Ethan. "We're on our way!"

And so they were, with only one question remaining. Would the battery hold out until they got to where they needed to go?

The LVR rattled and bumped over the Great Sync, moving from the beginning of time to the end of time, then continuing backward toward that point somewhere in between, when Olivia was poisoned by those dastardly Plexiwave henchmen.

"Are we there yet?" whined Simon after saying nothing for nearly thirty minutes, a personal record for him.

"Don't worry," said Ethan. "I'll let you know."

Jason looked above, checking on the viability of those all-important welds made to the ceiling panel. For now, Mr. Lumley's repair work seemed to be holding just fine. The issue of battery power, however, was another matter altogether. When another thirty minutes had passed, the lights in the cabin dimmed, and Professor Boxley checked the readout on the instrument panel.

"Now operating on reserve power," he said.

Ethan noted the date on the chronometer. "We've still got a ways to go. Let's hope we make it."

"We've got to make it," said Catherine. "Come on!"

"Getting close now," said Ethan after several minutes of silence.

The lights in the cabin dimmed further, then blinked twice, then went out altogether. With a slow groan, the LVR ground to a halt, leaving its passengers to sit in the dark and wonder.

"Well, Dad? Did we make it?" asked Jason.

Ethan's heavy sigh told them everything they needed to know. "We came up short, I'm afraid."

"How short?" asked Catherine, though it really didn't matter. Either way, they had arrived sometime after Olivia had been poisoned, and anytime after that was too late.

"According to the last reading I got from the chronometer, almost two years," said Ethan.

"Two years?" said Jason. He felt like kicking or punching

something. He also felt like crying, but he wasn't about to do that in front of Big. "So then, we're right back where we started?"

"It looks that way," said Ethan.

"So she's still dead," said Simon.

"Yes," said Ethan in a hoarse whisper. "She's . . . still dead." He buried his face in his arms, which rested on the control panel.

"So what do we do now?" asked Simon. The question was met only with silence. Big took Simon's hand and gave it a squeeze, and he leaned his troubled head against her shoulder. For some time, they all sat in silence, giving no thought to what they should do next because nothing seemed to matter anymore.

Finally, Ethan stood up as straight as the weight he carried would allow him. "According to the chronometer it's January 13th," he said. "Assuming we're still in the Northern Hemisphere, with no battery power we could freeze to death if we stay here. We have to find someplace warm for the night. In the morning, we'll figure out what to do about the battery."

They each grabbed one of the animal skins that Sullivan had given them, then Ethan opened the pod door and stepped out into the dark, cold winter air, with the others right behind him. Not only did they come up short by a couple of years, it seemed that they were also off on their location. The surrounding land was rocky, dry, and cracked, and looked nothing like the Cheesemans' old neighborhood, which was dotted with oak and elm trees, the tidy little houses surrounded by lush, green lawns.

"Where are we?" asked Jason.

"I'm not sure," said Ethan. "Somewhere in the southwestern United States would be my guess."

"Why is the southwest so cold?" said Simon, wrapping the animal skin around his shoulders.

"Because it's the desert," said Catherine. "The air is thinner and loses heat more rapidly."

"I suppose we should try to make a fire," said Ethan.

"Or," said Jason, "we could check out that light over there." Sure enough, far off in the distance in the direction Jason was pointing was a white light.

"Could be a house," said Professor Boxley.

"Or a doughnut shop," said Simon.

"That's absurd," said Catherine. "Who in their right mind would put a doughnut shop way out here in the middle of nowhere?"

"Someone who likes to eat leftover doughnuts," said Gravy-Face Roy.

The cold and weary travelers trudged across the dry, frozen ground toward the single white light. As they got closer, it soon became apparent that Professor Boxley was right, and Simon was disappointed. It was a house. In fact, you could say it was a mansion. The beautifully manicured grounds featured several fountains and a sculpture of two figures standing nearly eight feet tall. In the dark, they resembled some kind of hideous space creatures.

"What are those things?" Simon trembled.

"I think they're snails," said Catherine.

"I don't like this doughnut shop," said Gravy-Face Roy.

Ethan stopped in front of a steet sign. "Bumbleberry Lane," he muttered. "Why does that sound so familiar?"

"Because you love bumbleberry pie?" Jason suggested.

"Yes, that's probably it," said Ethan as he continued on, giving the sign one last quizzical look. But as they neared the mansion he stopped again, this time next to a mailbox at the end of the very long driveway. He realized then that it was not his love of bumbleberry pie that had made the street sign sound so familiar. It was something far more important and much more incredible.

"I don't believe it," said Ethan when he saw the name on the mailbox. "It can't be."

ADVICE ON GIVING ADVICE

As the highly successful founder, president, and vice president of the National Center for Unsolicited Advice, I would like to take a few moments to tell you how I went from living in a tiny one-bedroom apartment to living in a huge, 8,000 square-foot mansion. How did I do it? I moved back in with my parents.

It was while living there—and being advised on a daily basis that I needed to get off the couch and find a job—that I first developed the concept of unsolicited advice as a moneymaking venture.

And now, for a limited time only, I would like to share with you the keys to success in this exciting and rewarding field. Why pursue a career in unsolicited advice, you ask? (Even if you didn't ask, here's your answer.)

For one thing, there are no start-up fees, no products to buy, and there is no special training required. I assure you the same cannot be said of unsolicited dentistry, unsolicited dog grooming, or unsolicited wart removal (now illegal in all fifty states). When it comes to proffering words of wisdom to the unsuspecting, all you need to start you on your way to mega-riches is a willingness to be annoying.

Tooth Extraction
Wart Removal
Flea Bath
$1.00

Start small, with friends and family, advising them on what clothes to wear, how they should style their hair, and with whom they should associate. Before you know it, people will be paying you large sums of money just to butt out and mind your own business.

For more on this exciting and rewarding career, write to the NCUA for your deluxe information packet, which is absolutely free, plus $9.99 shipping and handling. If you prefer that your packet be shipped without being handled, please specify.

In the meantime, be advised that with this amazing opportunity comes great responsibility, because, though giving just the right advice can be quite beneficial to the recipient, giving the wrong advice can prove absolutely disastrous.

CHAPTER 13

It had been a particularly long week of doling out unsolicited advice to people the world over. It all started with a trip to Tangiers, where I advised the locals on some handy alternative uses for that cylindrical hat known as the fez. They make nice planters, for instance.

From there I was off to Tibet to meet with the Dalai Lama and advise him that he might do well to change his name to Dolly Llama and become a female country and western singer.

Next came a stopover in Washington DC, where I sat down with the president of the United States and offered suggestions on how to pay off the national debt, which, at that time, had just surpassed fourteen trillion dollars. To give you an idea of how much money that is, if you were to take fourteen trillion one-dollar bills and lay them end to end, you would be beaten and robbed in about six minutes.

Regardless, I advised the president that the debt could be reduced by selling advertising space on those very dollars. Seriously, who even knows what *Annuit Oceptis* means? Why not replace it—along with that goofy-looking one-eyed pyramid—with the words *I can't believe it's not butter,* or *I wish I were an Oscar Mayer weiner,* along with a coupon for thirty cents off on your next purchase?

I offered this advice free of charge, from one president to another, and I believe it was well received. After being escorted out by White House security, I hopped a cab to the airport and flew the NCUA corporate jet back to head-quarters.

Now, of course, the NCUA does employ a full-time pilot, the highly capable decorated war hero Captain Chuck "Cupcake" Baker, but I always prefer to be at the controls myself whenever possible. Flying, I find, can be quite relax-ing after a long day of telling other people what to do.

On these occasions, Captain Cupcake is likely to accuse me of being a control freak, pointing out my choice of careers as further evidence of this assertion. When he does make such comments, I am inclined to heartily disagree, then make him sit in back, where he cannot be heard.

Upon my return to the NCUA headquarters, I strode into my palatial office (I so enjoy a good stride) to find my longtime personal assistant, Flolene, who greeted me with a warm smile and a hot cup of tea.

"Welcome back, Dr. Soup," she said in that slow, sleepy Southern drawl. "I trust your trip went well."

"Quite," I said, taking a sip of the tea, brewed to perfec-tion as can only be done by a true Southerner. "A rousing success, though I must say the mosquitoes in Morocco are the size of Canadian geese." The mere mention of this reminded me of an especially nasty bite on my right elbow, and I had to grit my teeth to fight off the urge to scratch it. "Any mail of interest?"

Flolene knew better than to try to determine whether the mail would be of interest to me or not, and simply handed me the stack that had accumulated during my week abroad. Nothing terribly exciting. Plenty of bills, a few checks, a smattering of Christmas cards, and a coupon for one dollar off on a pizza that had cheese inserted into the crust, which was also made entirely of cheese. And, as always, there was no shortage of letters asking for advice on a large range of topics. Of course, when one actually *asks* for advice, that puts it firmly in the realm of the solicited variety, and so I promptly instructed Flolene to have those letters forwarded on to the NCSA, located somewhere in Iowa, I believe.

Weary from my travels, I summoned Hans, my driver for the past seventeen years, and had him bring the limo around. I mentioned to Hans that I should like to drive myself, as it always relaxes me after a long day of flying the corporate jet. He mumbled something about me being a control freak, or at least that's what it sounded like coming from the backseat.

It was quite late by the time I arrived at my sprawling mansion, known affectionately as Soup Manor. My elderly parents had long since gone off to bed, and I was greeted at the door by my loyal Jack Russell terrier, Kevin, whom I had adopted nine years earlier when I found out I was unable to have puppies.

All in all, Kevin had been a good dog over the years, though he did suffer occasional lapses in behavior, having once been kicked out of obedience school for telling the teacher that I had eaten his homework—which, for the record, I had not.

My two snails, Gooey and Squishy, on the other hand, were pets of exemplary character, and were accomplished athletes as well. Like my parents, they had also gone to bed early that evening, exhausted from their extensive training for the upcoming Iron Snail competition.

And so the mansion was quiet, and I seized the opportunity for some much-needed down time. In the kitchen, I opened the fridge and found that Mother had brewed up a large batch of her famous Spam® chowder, the most delicious thing one could ever hope to eat. Unfortunately, because the recipe is a closely guarded family secret, I am unable at this time to reveal the secret ingredient that gives this dish its special ham-like flavor.

I hungrily polished off two large bowls' worth, while Kevin ate three. I then retired to the sitting room, where I put on some classical music (Rossini, coincidentally) and settled into my chair by the fire with a delightful cabernet sauvignon and a good book, because, as they say, a good book is like a good friend. Well, good luck trying to find a book that will loan you money, bail you out of jail, or water your plants while you're on vacation. Or in jail.

A good book, I'm afraid, is nothing like a good friend, but reading one is a very agreeable experience. So I settled into my chair, cracked the spine, and tucked into it while Kevin curled up at my feet.

I had gotten only a few pages into the book and a few sips into the wine when, suddenly, the doorbell rang, causing Kevin to let out his standard woof, which came whenever any type of ringing, dinging, or buzzing noise was made anywhere. The ringing of the doorbell was doubly strange because the remote location of the mansion meant that we received very few unannounced visitors, and even fewer at such a late hour and in such cold weather.

I set my glass and the book aside. With Kevin on my heels, I walked to the front door and flipped on the porch light, then looked through the peephole. Personally, I've never found peepholes to be of much use. All they tell you is that someone with a disproportionately large forehead is standing on your stoop. In this case, it was several persons, and an odd-looking bunch at that, their elongated faces aside.

They say a picture is worth a thousand words. I'm not sure what a thousand words are worth, but I do know for a fact that you can't use them to buy a motor home. The picture that lay before my right eye, as I pressed it against the peephole, was a strange one, to say the least. For a moment, I feared that it might have been some type of hallucination brought on by those horrible Moroccan mosquitoes or as the result of the jet lag that was now setting in.

If they were Christmas carolers, it was awfully late for

them to be showing up at someone's door, and if they were trick-or-treaters, it was later still, though I must say they did somewhat look the part. One of the smaller members of the bunch appeared to be dressed as a Native American baseball player, complete with beaded braids, buckskin clothing, and a bright blue cap. Another of them sported some kind of crude puppet on his left hand. All of them were draped in animal pelts, and, if that weren't enough to pique my curiosity, there was also a hairless pink dog and a small brown fox.

I might very well have ignored this unlikely bunch and tiptoed back to my comfortable chair and my friendly book, but, being that it was the holiday season, I thought they may have been collecting for a needy cause, or that they themselves might be a needy cause. When I opened the door and caught a non-distorted look at my late-night visitors, I was shocked beyond belief.

"Sorry to barge in on you like this, Bertie," said a bespectacled man with a large bruise over his eye. The fact that this stranger at my door had just addressed me by my college nickname caused me no small amount of confusion.

"It's me," the man continued. "Ethan."

"Ethan Cheeseman?" I said, with equal degrees of befuddlement and delight. While Ethan's certainly was a memorable face, it took me a moment to try to make sense of the situation. Standing next to Ethan was an elderly man, along with that hairless dog and the brown fox, and a small brood of children. Or is it a *herd* of children? I must look that up.

Regardless, were they brood or herd or four-legged beast, I welcomed them all into my home, for I've had few friends in my life of the quality of Ethan Cheeseman.

Ethan and I had first met at Southwestern North Dakota State University, where we played football together for the SWNDSU Fighting Paper Clips. We pledged the same fraternity and were, for the first couple of years there, fairly inseparable. That is, until Ethan met the lovely Olivia Lodbrock. After that, none of us saw too much of him. In fact, the last time I had seen him in person was the day he made the very wise move of taking Olivia as his wife. I was only mildly offended when he chose that pretentious gadabout Chadwick Peabody to be his Best Man while I was forced to settle with being named *Most Improved*.

In the years that followed, Ethan and I made an attempt to keep in touch, but slowly fell out of contact the way people tend to do in a busy world such as this. While I was focused on starting a business, Ethan turned his attentions to starting a family. I could only surmise that the young people with him now were part of that family.

With a closer look I was also able to determine the identity of the elderly gentleman in the group. He was none other than Acorn Boxley, the esteemed physics professor at SWNDSU. Being that my field of study was in the humanities and not in the sciences, I had never had occasion to make the professor's acquaintance, but now was honored to do so.

"Ethan, old boy. What in heaven's name brings you here?" I said, offering him the secret fraternity handshake, which he rather clumsily returned. He never did seem to be too enthusiastic about the whole fraternity lifestyle. He'd always been more of an independent soul, a lone wolf, if you will. "Come in, come in before you all catch pneumonia."

"Wow. This sure is a big house," said the boy with the sock puppet, who I would soon learn was Simon, Ethan's youngest of three children.

"You can say that again," said the sock puppet I would soon come to know as Gravy-Face Roy.

"You all look a bit weary," I said. "Please have a seat on the chesterfield."

Young Simon, apparently unfamiliar with the word, tried to sit on the dog.

"No, no," I said. "That's Kevin. The chesterfield is the couch, or sofa if you prefer."

"I prefer the couch," Simon said, and promptly sat down on the sofa, with the others squeezing in beside him. Kevin, traumatized by nearly being sat upon, curled up at my feet and leveled a cautious stare at the four-legged interlopers in his living room.

"May I offer you a cup of tea?" I asked my surprise visitors. "Or perhaps a bowl of Spam® chowder?"

"No, thank you," said Jason. He looked a far cry from the baby picture on his birth announcement, which I'd been sent all those years ago. My, how the time had flown; for here was this person I had known only as an infant and only in photographic form, now sitting in my living room, shyly introducing me to his girlfriend, the pretty young woman named Big.

And though I'd never seen a photo of Catherine, it was clear beyond any doubt that she was the daughter of Ethan and Olivia. Smart as a whip, I could tell in a flash. And that beautiful auburn hair. It sparkled and shined just the way Olivia's had on her wedding day. Which, of course, prompted me to ask, "And how is Olivia?"

What I assumed to be a simple and entirely innocuous question seemed to cause Ethan great distress. He suddenly appeared more pale and exhausted than I had ever seen him look after all those grueling football practices.

"Didn't you get the postcards?" he asked.

"Postcards?" I said with consternation, for the last contact I'd had from Ethan or from any of the Cheesemans was that singular birth announcement some twelve years before. "I haven't received any postcards."

"I sent you postcards. Loads of them, to this address," Ethan said. "From the road, telling you about Olivia and how she was poisoned."

"Poisoned?" This awful news caused my knees to buckle, and I nearly fell back into my chair.

"Yes," said Ethan. "You've always had a certain way with words, and I wanted you to be the one to tell our story, in case anything were to happen to us before we were able to go back and save her life."

"This is the first I've heard of this dreadful occurrence."

"Well," said Ethan, with a disgusted shake of his head, "nothing else has gone right, so I guess it's possible that they all got lost in the mail somehow."

"That seems pretty unlikely," said Jason. "Maybe you sent them to the wrong address."

"Thirty-four-fifty Bumbleberry Lane," said Ethan. "Placitas, New Mexico."

"Wait a minute," said Catherine. She narrowed her eyes, as if doing a difficult math problem in her head. "You sent hundreds of postcards to this address, but they never arrived? Is it possible that they never got here because you haven't sent them yet?"

"I see what you're saying," said Jason. "And maybe you haven't sent them yet because it hasn't happened yet."

"Hasn't happened yet?" said Ethan. "What do you mean?"

"I mean," said Catherine, rising to her feet, "that maybe the chronometer on the LVR was wrong."

"It's unlikely," said Professor Boxley.

"More unlikely than a hundred postcards being lost in the mail?"

"I suppose it is possible that the chronometer was damaged when we crash-landed in 1668," said Ethan.

All this talk was beginning to make me feel as though I was in the presence of a group of crazy people. What was all this nonsense about chronometers and LVRs? If things seemed strange now, they were about to get a great deal stranger yet.

"Bertie," said Ethan excitedly. "What's today's date?"

"Why, it's December 13th," I said, assuming my friend was interested in how many shopping days remained until Christmas.

Ethan sprang to his feet, walked over, and took me by the arm. There was a slightly crazed look in his eye, and I began to develop concern for his personal well-being, and for my own as well. "That's the day before she was poisoned," he said. "The chronometer was wrong." And then, as I would later learn, came the truly important part. "And what year is it?"

Never before in all my days had anyone ever asked me what year it was. After all, there are very few reasons for someone to be unaware of the proper year. Being stranded in a location so remote that it had no calendar store would be one explanation. Suffering from amnesia would be another. And the only other reason that comes to mind for a person not knowing the calendar year is that that person has been traveling through time and has no idea where he has landed.

Individually, Ethan and Olivia were two of the most brilliant people I had ever met. Together they would certainly create a force to be reckoned with. But time travel? Was it really possible? I had no way of knowing for sure. But what I do know is that when I told Ethan what year it was, he practically exploded with enthusiasm, taking a triumphant punch at the air.

The others in my sitting room reacted in similar fashion, celebrating the news as if they'd just won the lottery or the Iron Snail competition.

"She's still alive," said Catherine. "She doesn't drink the coffee until tomorrow morning."

The children leaped to their feet and hugged one another. "Yes!" said Simon as he engaged in a double high five with Professor Boxley, forgetting that his left hand was currently occupied by a sock puppet.

"Ouch!" said Gravy-Face Roy.

"Your phone," said Ethan. "I need to borrow your phone."

I hurried off to retrieve the cordless phone, which always seemed to be somewhere one wouldn't expect. Once, I found it in the freezer, next to a half-empty carton of butterbrickle ice cream. This time I located it in the laundry hamper. I returned to the sitting room, where I was mobbed like a rock star.

"I want to talk to her too," said Simon.

"Don't worry, you'll get a chance," said Ethan. "You'll all get a chance." I handed my friend the phone. He stared at the keypad and did nothing else. "Does anyone remember our phone number?"

"I do," said Catherine, who had more room in her oversized brain for such things.

Ethan quickly dialed the number. So shaky were his hands that he had to hang up and start over twice before getting the number right. "It's ringing," he whispered finally.

"Hello?" came the sleepy voice on the other end.

"Olivia," Ethan practically shouted. He covered the phone and whispered to his children, as if what he was about to say next was a closely guarded secret to which Olivia herself was not privy. "She's alive."

"Hello? Who is this?" asked Olivia.

"It's me, Ethan."

"What?" said Olivia. "Listen, I don't know who you are, but if you call here again I'm going to the police." The line went dead, and Ethan stared at the phone before quickly hitting redial, but the call went right to voice mail.

"What's wrong, Dad?" asked Simon. "What happened?"

"I think she unplugged the phone. Darn it. I should have known she wouldn't believe me. After all, why should she? I think the only way to convince her is to do so in person. Bertie, what time is it?"

I looked across the room and consulted the grandfather clock, which had been a gift from my grandmother on my father's side. "Well," I began, "according to my grandmother's grandfather clock, it's nearly eleven thirty, though it does tend to run a bit slow. Just like my grandmother."

My little joke, which I thought quite the zinger, was unceremoniously ignored by all. Instead, a sense of panic seemed to rip through the room.

"Olivia gets up at five every morning," said Ethan. "The first thing she does is drink her coffee. That's how they poisoned her. By putting it in her coffee. That gives us just five and a half hours to get there."

This was indeed a problem, because *there*, as it turns out, was quite far away from *here*, and it was about to get a lot farther when Catherine said, "Correct me if I'm wrong, but isn't there a two-hour time difference?"

"That's right," said Ethan. "That gives us just three and a half hours."

"We could wait until tomorrow," Professor Boxley suggested. "That would give us time to fix the battery on the LVR, and we could go back a few days into the past, which would give us plenty of time to get there."

"And let her drink poison again?" said Ethan. "Not a chance. Besides, if we wait, something could go wrong. It's too risky. This might be our only opportunity, and we've got to take it."

"I agree," said Jason. "But how do we get there? We'd need a rocket ship to make it in time."

And then, something occurred to me. "Yes, a rocket ship," I said. "Or a corporate jet."

"Corporate jet?" said Ethan, his eyes suddenly filled with hope. "What corporate jet?"

"The NCUA corporate jet," I announced. "I can get you there in about three hours if all goes well."

Of course, this did not include travel time to and from each airport, but it was the best I could do, and I strongly advised the Cheesemans that my plan was our absolute best hope for success. "Quick, to the limo," I said, feeling ever so slightly like Batman. Then suddenly it occurred to me to do a head count. The NCUA corporate jet is a bit on the smaller side and seats only a half dozen, including the pilot and copilot. I explained that one of them would have to stay behind, and it was pretty much between the two non-Cheesemans, Professor Boxley and Big.

"I'll stay," Professor Boxley bravely volunteered.

"Thanks," said Big, though, by the way she looked at

Jason, I would bet there's no way she would have let him board that plane without her.

With precious minutes ticking away, I quickly explained to the professor where he could find the guest room and advised him that should he encounter my elderly parents the following morning, he should simply pretend to be me. "Odds are, they won't know the difference," I said. "If that doesn't work, tell them you're there to fix the phonograph."

"Good luck, Ethan," the professor said, offering Ethan a regular, non-secret handshake. "And don't worry. I know you'll make it."

"Thanks, Professor," said Ethan. "Thanks for everything."

Outside, we raced to the limo. Big, who apparently came from modest means and had never before seen a limo up close, said, "What is this thing?"

"It's a car," said Jason. "Remember? I told you about them. It's okay, get in." Big, the other humans, and the animals all piled into the limo. Everyone, that is, but young Simon, who stood outside the car while the others beckoned him inward.

"Simon, let's go," said Ethan. "What's wrong?"

Simon remained silent, but Gravy-Face Roy said, "It's just that . . . you see, I'm afraid of flying."

"Your puppet is more than welcome to stay here with the professor," I said, not realizing that young Simon was using Gravy-Face Roy to voice his own concerns about air travel.

"It'll be okay, Simon," said Mr. Cheeseman. "It's no different than riding in the LVR, really."

Simon looked uncertain, but his doubt was no match for the faith he had in his father. He climbed into the limo, buckled up, and we set out at breakneck speed for the airport.

ADVICE FOR NERVOUS FLIERS

Ever since man first looked to the heavens, he has dreamed of soaring through the sky while nibbling on a small bag of honey-roasted peanuts.

Today, this dream is a reality thanks to the Wright brothers, who were busy perfecting the airplane while the Parker Brothers were off creating *Monopoly* and the Ringling Brothers committed themselves to inventing the circus.

These days we take flying for granted, though if I might be so bold, let me say that air travel is far and away the best mode of transportation. I know I'm taking a risk saying that, considering what happened to Archduke Ferdinand after making a similar statement. Still, the facts remain that flying is safer than driving, it's faster than a speeding locomotive, and it requires a great deal less balance than riding a unicycle (in my opinion, the second-best way to travel).

Still, there are those who are reluctant to board an airplane, stating that, "If man were meant to fly, he would have been born with wings, and an overhead compartment for his carry-on bags." These people are known as *nervous fliers* and are easily identified by their uncontrollable weeping whenever the plane hits a little unexpected turbulence.

Yes, it's true that air travel can be quite bumpy in rough weather, which is why most major airlines require that you keep your seat belt buckled at all times while seated on the airplane. However, you will notice there is no seat belt in the airplane lavatory, which is odd, considering that this is one place where you might want to be strapped into your seat during some heavy-duty turbulence.

And though sometimes unnerving, turbulence is nothing to worry about and is no different than driving your car (or unicycle) down a very bumpy road, at thirty thousand feet, with two tons of jet fuel directly beneath you. So you see, flying is the best way to get from point A to point B, and I strongly advise you to embrace it, especially if your point B is a thousand miles away and you have only three hours to get there.

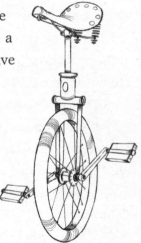

CHAPTER 14

For the record, riding in a limousine, like flying in an airplane, is generally a very comfortable mode of transportation, unless you are speeding along gravel-covered back roads and taking shortcuts through hay fields. Then, it can be a very turbulent ride.

"Are you sure this is the right way?" shouted Catherine from the backseat, her head coming dangerously close to the ceiling with each bounce and every bump as we made our way across the muddy ground.

"Trust me, I know exactly what I'm doing," I said.

"Look out!" said Ethan.

"Mooo," said the cow I almost ran over but didn't, thanks to a beautifully executed last-minute swerve.

The car jounced along, then took to the air as it left the hay field, flying up the shoulder of the main road like a ramp before landing with the horrible screech of rubber hitting pavement and the sparks of . . . some metal car part (I've never claimed to be a mechanic) hitting that same pavement.

I cranked the wheel hard to the right in an effort to get the car going in the same direction as the road, which I find is the most efficacious use of roads. The back end swung around and the spinning tires spat out gravel from the opposite shoulder. When they finally caught blacktop, the car lurched forward with a chirp and sped down the main road toward the airport.

Suddenly, Pinky began growling a very low and steady growl. "What's the matter? Is there a problem with your dog?" I asked.

"She's psychic," said Jason. "She growls whenever she senses danger."

As I saw nothing to cause alarm, I could only conclude that the silly beast considered my driving to be a danger worth growling at.

"Oh, is that all," I said, with a sigh of relief. "For a moment I was afraid she might be on the verge of doing something unsavory in the car. I just had the interior detailed last week. Anyway, I can assure you there's no danger to worry about. Everything is under control. However, there is one small wrinkle to consider."

"How small?" asked Ethan.

"And how wrinkly?" asked Gravy-Face Roy.

"Quite small and just a tad on the wrinkled side," I said as we rocketed past a sign indicating we were in an area where stick figures frequently crossed the road. "This is a rather small town, as you may have noticed, and I'm afraid the airport closes at midnight."

"Then why are we going there if we can't even fly out?" asked Catherine.

"Oh, I didn't say we couldn't fly out. I just said the airport was closed. It'll just make flying out a bit more . . . challenging."

"But isn't that illegal?" asked Jason.

"Only if you get caught," I hollered over my shoulder while my eyes remained focused on the dark, curvy asphalt coming toward me at a highly illegal rate of speed.

"But if you do get caught, you could lose your pilot's license," said Simon.

"Pilot's license?" I scoffed.

This seemed to cause a noticeable increase in the already high level of tension in the air. "You do have a pilot's license," said Ethan pointedly.

"Do you need a license to ride a bicycle?" I responded. "Or a lawn mower? Why should an airplane be any different?"

"Uh, because it travels thirty thousand feet above the ground," said Jason, apparently a bit skeptical as to my aeronautic prowess.

"Licenses are overrated," I opined. "My dog, Kevin, has a license, and he couldn't fly a plane if his life depended on it. I, on the other hand, am an excellent pilot and have never been involved in a fatal crash."

"What do you mean you've never been involved in a *fatal* crash?" asked Catherine.

I did not have time to answer the young girl's question

because, at that very moment, my rearview mirror became filled with flashing blue and red lights.

"A policeman," I said with exasperation. "What is a policeman doing out and about at this hour?"

My passengers all turned and looked out the back window to confirm that, yes, a police cruiser was hot on our trail, its lights blazing, its siren blaring.

"You should probably pull over," said Simon. "If you don't, he might shoot us."

"I don't think he'll shoot us," said Jason. "But you probably should pull over anyway, Dr. Soup. Otherwise you could lose your driver's license."

"Driver's license?" I scoffed as I made a hard right onto a dirt road, which I had intended to take anyway.

"Maybe if you pull over and explain the situation to him, he'll give us a police escort," said Catherine.

"I don't think so," I replied. "The local police department seemed to take offense when I recently advised them that they were in desperate need of some additional training and special dietary restrictions."

I killed the lights and took a hairpin turn onto a smaller dirt road, then quickly turned off that road and sped across a rutabaga farm, which is even bumpier than a hay field, if you can imagine. A quick check of my mirror confirmed that I had lost my pursuer. I'm not one to say I told you so, but it seems as though the local police department might have done well to heed my advice.

On the other side of that rutabaga farm sat the airport, closed for the night and quiet as a graveyard. I stopped the limo next to a chain-link fence that ran astride the runway. Spiraling along the top of the fence was a rather nasty-looking stretch of barbed wire, mortal enemy to pants everywhere.

"Okay, let's go," I commanded, tiny clouds of steam escaping from my mouth and into the frigid December air with every word. I climbed out of the car and my passengers followed, a bit too tentatively for my liking. I opened the trunk of the limo and pulled out a pair of bolt cutters, because you never know when you're going to have to break into an airport.

Working quickly, I snapped enough links of the fence that it could be peeled back, allowing us to squeeze through and to avoid the barbed wire altogether.

"This way," I said, sprinting across a patch of grass toward the NCUA corporate jet, which was known affectionately as the Concorde Grape. It had earned its nickname because of its dark purple paint job, which was a holdover from when it had served as the corporate jet for the National Eggplant Association.

"Don't worry," I said to an obviously nervous Simon as I unlocked the hatch and pulled it open. "Flying is the safest form of travel. Unless, of course, you do so without filing a flight plan; then it can get a bit dicey. Still, not to worry."

"What is this thing?" asked Big, and I began to wonder just what type of sheltered existence the girl had lived up to this point.

"This is an airplane," said Jason. "Remember, I told you

about the giant birds that fly through the sky? This is one of them."

As we boarded the plane, Jason informed me that Big was from the year 1668, and suddenly everything made perfect sense. Wait a minute, what am I saying? This made no sense at all, but there was no time to dwell upon it.

When all had buckled up for the ride ahead and the animals had climbed into awaiting laps, I pulled the hatch closed and took my seat in the cockpit, with Ethan taking the copilot's seat. Believe me when I say there's nothing in this world quite so satisfying as firing up a jet engine. The sheer power that one can summon with the simple press of a button is awe-inspiring, to say the least.

"I don't mean to insult you," said Ethan as we began our taxi to the runway, "but my entire family is aboard this plane. Are you absolutely sure you know what you're doing?"

"Listen, Einstein," I said, which was not a smart-aleck remark, but rather Ethan's nickname in college. *Einstein Cheeseman* we called him, because of the fact that he rarely found time to comb his hair. "You're more likely to be struck by lightning than to be involved in a plane crash."

Just then, a bolt of lightning shot across the sky, followed by a sharp crack of thunder. "See?" I said. "Now do you trust me?"

Good old Einstein stuttered something about how that did not prove anything, but my concentration was consumed by the task of taking off on a runway with no lights.

As the Concorde Grape careened down the tarmac,

another charge of lightning shivered across the sky, affording me a good view of the runway and alerting me to the fact that it was unexpectedly about to end.

"Uh-oh," I said, which is something that should never be uttered by a pilot whose credentials and abilities are in question.

"Uh-oh?" Ethan repeated.

I pulled back on the stick, and the plane took to the stormy sky.

You have to understand how exciting this was for me. Of all the times I had flown the Concorde Grape, I had never done so with passengers in the back, and had never before had cause to use the P.A. system.

"Good evening from the cockpit, ladies and gentlemen," I said in my deepest, most piloty voice. "This is your captain, Dr. Cuthbert Soup. I'll be assisted today by my copilot, Ethan Cheeseman, and we'll be cruising at an altitude of anywhere between twenty-five and thirty thousand feet, depending on where the lightning is. Barring any unexpected delays, we should be arriving at our destination in approximately two hours and fifty-five minutes, local time 4:51 a.m."

"That's cutting it close," said Ethan.

"Sorry," I replied. "If it hadn't been for that cop I would've been able to stay on the main road longer. If we get a good tailwind, we can probably make up a little time."

As luck would have it, we did not get a tailwind, but we did get wind and plenty of it to go along with the thunder and lightning that menaced the skies that night. What followed was one of the bumpiest flights I've ever had the displeasure of being a party to. How my passengers in back were handling the turbulent ride I couldn't be sure, but I did notice that my copilot was, for most of the flight, pale as a vampire's ghost. Still, he kept his wits about him and his eyes on the chronometer.

"I don't know," he said. "Our house is a good thirty-minute drive from the airport."

"Airport?" I said. "We haven't filed a flight plan, so technically we're not cleared to land at the airport, I'm afraid. But my GPS is telling me that the local university has a very nice soccer field. Artificial turf, I believe."

"You're going to land on a soccer field?"

"Actually, I'm going to *try* to land on a soccer field. We'll see how it goes. The good news is it's just a ten-minute walk from your house. Or a six-minute jog. Or a four-minute sprint."

One way in which soccer fields are not at all like landing strips is that they are not nearly as long. Due to this one little factor, our landing would require a very steep descent and a fair amount of luck. Still, I looked forward to the challenge and to saying that I may be the only person to have ever completed a touchdown on a soccer field.

Before an actual attempt at landing, I would first have to perform a flyover, a low pass over the makeshift airstrip. It was important to know whether there were hazards near the field, such as power lines, tall trees, or policemen. Luckily, the skies had cleared and our view of the field was sharp and unobstructed as we dropped in for a closer look.

"No problem," I said, with more confidence in my voice than in my gut.

I took it back up and made a sharp bank left, circling over houses where, undoubtedly, the sleepy residents were curious as to why a jet airplane was buzzing overhead at such a ridiculously early hour. I thought it best to inform my passengers of the latest developments to prepare them for the sudden drop that awaited them, and I once more switched on the intercom.

"Good morning from the cockpit, ladies and gentlemen. We're currently at one thousand feet, dropping to zero feet in the next thirty seconds or so. Please make sure that your seat belts are securely fastened and that your pockets are free of all sharp objects or anything that might explode on impact."

For the record, this was not the first time I had attempted an unconventional landing such as this. Once, when flying from Montreal to Albuquerque, one of the Concorde Grape's engines caught fire, forcing me to make an unscheduled stop in a Kansas cornfield. No one was hurt, but the heat from the fire did result in about six hundred pounds of popcorn, which is why I always make sure the Concorde Grape is well stocked with plenty of salted butter.

Compared to that little episode, this landing would be a six-hundred-pound piece of cake. I lowered the nose, taking a sharp trajectory toward the ground. We dropped from a thousand feet to a hundred feet in just seconds.

"Pull up!" yelled Ethan as the earth raced up to meet us. "Pull up!"

He was right. I pulled back hard on the stick and the plane leveled out just as the wheels hit the artificial turf, giving us all a wicked jolt. Quickly, I activated the reverse thrusters and hit the brakes as hard as I could without losing control of the aircraft. The sudden force caused Ethan to lurch forward in his seat, while I myself had to fight to remain in position to guide the speeding plane along the ground.

The end of the field was coming up fast, and though the plane had slowed considerably, we were still a long way from coming to a complete and final stop. Beyond the field was a road, and across that road was a track-and-field practice facility.

We reached the end of the soccer field and the plane skipped over the road, narrowly missing a parked car and a *No Parking* sign, then bounded onto the infield of the track, where, finally, we crawled to a stop. Ethan and I sat, unable to speak. I wondered how the children had come through the harrowing experience. I imagined they were nothing less than traumatized. Suddenly, there was a thumping on the cabin door. My face and hands mottled with beads of cold sweat, I peeled myself off the captain's chair and opened the cockpit to find Catherine and the other children standing at the entrance.

"What time is it?" she demanded. Traumatized indeed. I forgot that these children were the spawn of Ethan and Olivia Cheeseman.

"It's 5:05," I said with a quick check of the cockpit chronometer.

"Five after five?" exclaimed Jason.

"Yes," I confirmed. "I strongly advise you to run like the wind." As quickly as I could, I opened and lowered the door, the inside of which served as a stairwell to the ground. My passengers leaped from the aircraft one by one, except for Simon and Gravy-Face Roy, who leaped two by two. The others, Jason, Catherine, Big, Pinky, and Digs, hit the frozen ground and took off in a desperate sprint against time.

"Thanks, Bertie," said Ethan over his shoulder as he raced off after the others and never looked back.

"Good luck!" I called. "Let me know how it turns out!" I watched Ethan disappear into the darkness just as suddenly as he had shown up on my doorstep only four hours before. Then I looked at that giant purple jet plane parked on the grass in the middle of a university sports center a thousand miles from my home and thought, "Now what?"

CHAPTER 15

They say that the early bird catches the worm, whereas birds that are later to rise must be content with eating birdseed, bread crumbs, and fat, lazy worms who also enjoy sleeping in. Olivia Cheeseman was an early bird by nature. She rarely slept past five o'clock, and this morning she had been awake for hours after being jostled from unconciousness by a crank phone call.

She lay next to her snoring husband, thinking. But it wasn't the thought of bread crumbs or birdseed that filled her mind; she had remained quite disturbed by the strange phone call and the questionable people who had visited her house in recent days. She feared for the safety of her family.

Two government agents dressed all in gray had shown up at the front door and strongly suggested that she and her husband hand over the yet-to-be-finished LVR. They should do so, the men explained, for their own protection from those who might be willing to do anything to get their hands on it.

While she and Ethan had been out celebrating their

wedding anniversary, another strange man came to the house claiming to be selling vacuum cleaners door-to-door, which sounded entirely plausible, except for the fact that the man spoke in a strange accent and was accompanied by a monkey.

But the most unnerving of all the occurrences was when she and Ethan returned home from dropping the children off at school to find a long white limousine parked out front. Upon entering the house, they were startled and frightened to find, sitting in their living room, a large man with rings on each of his meaty fingers and a small woman with fingers as thin and bony as the man's were thick and meaty.

The woman announced that they worked for Plexiwave and that they were there with the purpose of offering high-paying jobs to Ethan and Olivia in exchange for the LVR and the secret codes necessary to operate it. To further entice the two scientists, the woman instructed the ring-fingered man to open and display the contents of a briefcase he was holding. It was full of cash; two million dollars, to be exact.

Some people might have salivated at the sight of so much money. The fact that it came from a company responsible for manufacturing deadly weapons, which had killed millions of people around the world, made Olivia nauseous, and she angrily ordered the intruders out of her house.

What made these multiple encounters all the more strange was that Ethan and Olivia had told no one, not even their own children, that they were working on a device that could very well enable time travel. Still, somehow, these strange visitors seemed to know all about the LVR.

She watched the digital readout on the nightstand clock snap from 4:59 to 5:00. She sat up and swung her legs over the edge of the bed. She grabbed her robe from a hook on the back of the door and quietly slipped out of the room.

She walked to the front door, as she did every morning, with the intention of bringing in the daily newspaper. For the first time ever, she changed her routine, deciding to leave the paper for later, when the sun would take away the darkness and all of the unknown that goes with it.

She flipped on the kitchen light and, with squinting eyes, fetched her coffee from the pantry. From the drawer below the coffeemaker, she retrieved a filter that, unfortunately, would do nothing to filter out the poison with which the coffee had been laced.

Olivia liked her coffee strong, and she loaded up the filter with several heaping spoonfuls of the ground, tainted beans. She added the water and hit the start button. The clock on the coffeemaker told her it was 5:05.

Jason felt as if his heart might pop right out of his chest, the blood pounding in his ears, his feet pounding the frozen earth as he sprinted toward the house he had called home for the first twelve years of his life. Closely on his heels were Catherine and Ethan, with Big, Digs, and Pinky lagging behind to stay with Simon, who had no hope of keeping pace with the group.

Though it had been two years, Jason had no problem remembering the quickest route to the house. Like an Olympian, he hurdled a short picket fence that encircled the front yard of the Baldersons' house on Musgrave Street. He ignored the *Beware of Dog* sign on the back gate, emboldened by the knowledge that the dog of which he was to beware was a fourteen-year-old schnauzer named Muffin with bad teeth and irritable bowel syndrome.

Jason raced through the backyard and scaled the much taller fence, paying no attention to the fact that he had, in the process, scraped his left forearm raw on the rough, unfinished wood. He felt no pain, only the sting of frustration from not being able to will his legs to go any faster.

As he sped along the gravel surface, he thought nothing of the dark blue sports car parked at the end of the alley. He thought of one thing only: the time. Finally, he arrived at his former house, and from a full run he jumped and took hold of the top of the fence. He pulled himself up and was aghast to see, projected by the kitchen light onto the curtains, a very familiar silhouette of a very familiar person. And in that silhouette's hand was what appeared to be a silhouette cup of coffee.

As the silhouette cup of coffee moved closer to the silhouette person's mouth, Jason stood on top of the fence, trying to maintain his balance while retrieving from his pocket the baseball Sullivan had given him. From his wobbly position atop the fence, he gripped the baseball, reared back, and . . . slipped.

His chin caught the fence on the way to the ground,

snapping his neck back and knocking him nearly senseless. He tasted blood, and realized a large gash had been opened across his bottom lip by his very own teeth. He opened his eyes to see the baseball rolling slowly down the alley toward his sister as she rumbled his way, pumping her arms and legs like a locomotive at full steam.

"The ball," Jason managed to garble with his swollen lower lip. "Throw it!"

Catherine spotted the autographed baseball lying at her feet. She picked it up and, with all her might, heaved it over the fence toward the house as Jason watched with blurred vision and listened with ringing ears. Long and painful seconds passed before finally the wonderful sound of breaking glass filled the air. Catherine had smashed the kitchen window, but had she done it in time? Jason pushed his belly from the ground and rose to his hands and knees. "Go," he said.

Without hesitation, Catherine took a running start, planted her foot in the middle of her injured brother's spine, and launched herself to the top of the fence. She pulled up, swung her legs over, and dropped into her own backyard next to the swing set on which she had experienced her very first under-duck.

Seconds later, Ethan ran up to find his elder son lying in the alley, his chin covered in blood. "I'm okay," Jason mumbled. "Go on." As Ethan pulled himself over the fence, he saw Catherine racing toward the back patio.

By now lights had started to come on inside the house. Still half-asleep, Ethan's younger double ran from the bedroom to find his wife with the kitchen phone to her ear. Right on his heels was Pinky, a full two years (or fourteen dog years) younger, and sporting a full coat of fur.

"What happened?" asked Ethan breathlessly. "What's going on?"

He looked down to see that the floor at Olivia's feet was littered with broken glass, a baseball, a shattered mug, and approximately six ounces of coffee, or, roughly, one full cup. Because Pinky had not yet developed psychic powers, the incident had come completely without warning.

"Someone threw something through the window," Olivia said in an unsteady voice. "I'm calling the police."

Before she could dial those three familiar numbers, there came a pounding on the kitchen door, accompanied by a voice that was awfully, but not quite entirely, familiar.

"Mom," said the voice. "It's me. Open the door!"

Olivia looked at Ethan. Was it a trick? After all, wasn't Catherine fast asleep in her room down the hall? "Careful," said Ethan as Olivia moved to the kitchen door and pulled back the curtain, only to be greeted by a most unusual sight. It was Catherine. Or was it? Though the resemblance was remarkable, this Catherine was taller, more mature-looking, and had much shorter hair. The young girl's eyes were filled with tears.

But was the girl real? Had the evil geniuses of Plexiwave somehow managed to manufacture a robotic version of her daughter in an effort to trick her into opening the door? "Mom, please," she cried. At that moment Olivia's maternal instincts overpowered her fears and suspicions, and she flung the door open. The short-haired girl on the back porch rushed in and immediately wrapped her arms tightly around Olivia's waist. The force of Catherine's hug caused Olivia to stumble back into the kitchen before finally regaining her balance. She looked to Ethan, but found no comfort in his equally confused face. She reached up and ran her hand gently across the girl's soft auburn hair.

Catherine sobbed at the long-awaited touch of the mother she hadn't seen since her death two years ago. "You're alive," she said, pulling away just far enough to get a look at Olivia's face. "You're alive again." Catherine's sobs turned to laughter, pure joy escaping from her body. For Olivia, there was no mistaking. That was definitely Catherine's laugh.

"Catherine?" she said. "Is it really you?"

"It's me, Mom," she said. "I came here from the future."

"From the future?" said Olivia. "What are you saying?"

"Oh my goodness," said Ethan, rising to his feet. His jaw went slack. "I think what she's saying is that the LVR works."

"It sure does," came a familiar voice from the doorway. The voice belonged to Ethan Cheeseman—the other Ethan Cheeseman, older by two years and several tons of stress, which seemed to vanish the minute he laid eyes on his wife. Unshowered and without makeup, her hair a tangled mess, she was, without a doubt, the most beautiful thing he had ever seen.

"I'm confused," said Olivia. "What's going on?"

"It's true," said Catherine. "The LVR works. That's how we got here from two years into the future."

Something suddenly occurred to Olivia. She looked at the younger Ethan, then at the older. "Wait a minute. That really was you on the phone last night."

"It was," said Ethan. "I'm sorry if I startled you. I don't blame you for hanging up on me."

"This is unbelievable," said Ethan the younger.

"Believe it," replied the senior Ethan. "Now if you'll excuse me, I've been waiting for two years to do this." He walked across the kitchen floor, took Olivia in his arms, and kissed her with a passion she hadn't experienced in far too long a time. The younger Ethan looked on with bemusement and, if he were to be completely honest, a good deal of jealousy. After all, another man was kissing his wife, even if that other man did happen to be himself.

"I've missed you so much," said Ethan to his flabbergasted but very much alive wife.

"I . . . I don't know what to say," Olivia stammered. She looked apologetically at her husband, who breathed a visible sigh of relief when his other self finally broke the embrace with his wife. The older Ethan walked over to the younger and extended his hand.

"Ethan Cheeseman," said Ethan.

"Yes, I know," said Ethan. "Nice to meet you." The two men shook hands and chuckled at the absurdity of the situation.

Gasping for breath, eight-year-old Simon ran up the

stairs to the back porch and into the kitchen. The boy practically flew into the room and jumped into his mother's arms. Between heaving sobs of jubilation he blubbered the same words Catherine had. "You're alive," he said. "You're really alive."

"Of course I'm alive," said Olivia. "I don't understand. What's going on?"

"Plexiwave," said Catherine. "They poisoned your coffee."

"And you died," added Simon, wiping his teary eyes and his runny nose on his mother's robe.

Olivia looked at the shattered coffee mug scattered about on the wet tile floor, suddenly realizing how close she had come to death. "So then, you came here from the future to save me?"

"That's right," said Ethan.

"But what about Jason? Where's Jason?"

"I'm right here," came the garbled reply as Jason walked into the kitchen with Big's help and with Digs and Pinky following right behind.

"You're hurt," said Olivia. She hugged and kissed her son, then helped him shuffle over to the kitchen table.

"I slipped off the fence," said Jason, dabbing at his bloody lip with his shirtsleeve. "But I'm okay." Olivia pulled a chair back, and with Big's assistance, Jason lowered himself onto it.

"Could you get some ice, Ethan?" Olivia instructed while examining Jason's badly split lip.

For a moment, the two Ethans just looked at each other before the younger of them said, "Sure," and hurried over to the fridge.

"You're so tall," Olivia said to Jason, pushing the long black curls away from his eyes. "And you have a mustache. And you have . . ." She looked at Big for the first time. "A girlfriend?"

"This is Big," said Jason. "She's from 1668."

"Hi," said Big with a shy smile.

"It's lovely to meet you," said Olivia, returning the smile. "Welcome to the twenty-first century." She laughed to herself at the idea of one of her offspring being old enough to have a girlfriend. Adults are fond of saying children grow up so fast, but rarely does a mother witness them age by two full years overnight.

Ethan brought over a small bundle of ice cubes wrapped in a wet washcloth and handed them to Jason. Jason pressed the cloth to his swollen lip and winced at the sting of it.

"Will you knit me a sock puppet named Steve?" asked Simon, refusing to let go of his mother's robe. "Please?"

"You saved my life," said Olivia, taking the opportunity to reach down and scruff up Simon's spiky hair. "I'll knit you a sock puppet named anything you like. Then you can get rid of that dirty old thing."

"It's not dirt," said Gravy-Face Roy. "It's gravy." Just then, Olivia noticed the presence in her kitchen of a small brown fox and what appeared to be a dog without hair.

"Why is there a fox in my kitchen?" she asked.

"That's Digs," said Jason. "He's Big's traveling companion."

"Okay," she said. "But what the heck is that thing?"

"That's Pinky," said Simon. "Don't you recognize her?"

"She lost all her hair when she drank your medicine out of the toilet," Jason explained.

"And she developed psychic powers too," added Catherine. "She's saved our lives many times over the last two years."

"It *is* Pinky, isn't it?" said Olivia upon a closer look. She gave the dog a good scratch behind the ears, and the younger Pinky scurried beneath the kitchen table with a yip and a whimper.

"It's okay, Pinky," said Simon reassuringly. "It's just you in the future, that's all."

The Cheeseman children were generally quite heavy sleepers, but all the commotion was bound to wake them eventually. The first to wander down the hall to see what all the fuss was about was Catherine. To Ethan and Olivia, the sudden appearance of slightly older versions of their entire family made sense, to a certain degree. After all, they had been working on a machine designed to transport people through time. But for Catherine, who knew only that her parents had been working on another one of their crazy inventions, the sight of herself standing in her very own kitchen was nothing less than mind-boggling, which was saying a lot, considering she possessed a mind that was not easily boggled.

"What's going on?"

For a moment, the two Catherines sized each other up. The older Catherine smiled and looked at her younger self with envy. The long-haired ten-year-old had lived a fairly idyllic life, having never known the heartache and stress that her older self had endured over the past two years on the run. "Hi," said the older Catherine to the younger with a warm smile. She felt protective of her, as if she were a younger sister; and in a strange way, that's exactly what she was.

"Who are all these people?" Catherine asked no one in particular. "They look just like . . ."

"That's because they are," her father said, draping his arm across her shoulders. "They're us. They've come here from the future."

"Okay," said Catherine flatly. "Apparently I'm still asleep, because this is one crazy dream. I'll be going back to bed now." She turned and started back down the hall when Jason stumbled out of his bedroom and nearly ran into her.

"What's all the noise out here?" he asked, rubbing his eyes.

"Oh, it's just a dream," said Catherine. "Go back to bed."

"Oh, okay," said Jason. He turned and took a step back, then stopped and turned again. It often happens in dreams that people you know will make a guest appearance, but will look slightly different from their actual selves. When relating the details of a dream to someone, it is not uncommon to say, "I had this dream last night. You were in it, but you were nine feet tall with two heads, four sideburns, and an Irish accent."

Never before had this seemed more true to Jason as he scanned the faces in the room looking back at him. In addition to a pretty girl dressed all in buckskin and a fox sniffing around the kitchen looking for crumbs, there were also slightly less than exact doubles of everyone but his mother. He thought the boy with the patchy teenage mustache bore a striking resemblance to himself, but this boy was older, taller, his eyes filled with a wisdom that Jason himself lacked. "This isn't a dream, is it?" asked Jason.

"It's not a dream," said Olivia. "Now, I know this might be hard for you kids to understand, but, you know that device your father and I have been working on for the past couple of years?"

"The one that was so secret you wouldn't tell us what it was?" said Catherine.

"Right," said Ethan the younger. "Well, we can tell you now. It's a time machine."

"A time machine?" said Catherine skeptically.

"Yes," said Olivia. "And, apparently, it works."

"But if they're here from the future," said Jason, "then where's our future mom?"

Ethan looked at his wife, then back at the younger Jason. His voice cracked as he spoke. "She . . . she died, I'm afraid."

"Died?" gasped Catherine.

"Yes," Ethan confirmed. "Poisoned, to be exact. That's why we had to come back. To save her. But she's still not out of danger. None of us are. Because of this time machine, we're all at risk from those who would do anything to get their hands on it."

This was a lot of information to process at such a ridiculously early hour. "So let me get this straight," said Jason. "You guys are us in a couple of years?"

"That's right," said the older Catherine.

Jason shook his head and rubbed the back of his neck. In doing so, he spied the baseball lying on the floor. He picked it up and immediately took notice of the signature it bore. "Why is there a baseball autographed by me sitting on our kitchen floor?"

"Because," said Jason, removing the pack of ice from his lip, "you and I are only the second person to have ever pitched a no-hitter in the World Series."

"We are? Seriously?" said Jason, rolling the ball around in his right palm.

"Seriously," said Jason.

"Awesome," said Jason. "But that can't happen until we're old enough to play in the majors. So where'd you get the ball?"

"Got it from Simon's grandson."

Jason looked at his little brother, now only four years his junior. "Simon is a grandfather?"

"He sure is," boasted Gravy-Face Roy. "And a world famous, award-winning novelist."

As if on cue, the younger Simon trudged out from his bedroom and into the kitchen, already chewing the massive wad of bubble gum he kept on his bedpost each night while he slept. "Can we open presents now?" he asked, his eyes at a mere fraction of their full openness.

"It's not Christmas yet," said Olivia.

"Well, if it's not Christmas, then why are we up so early?"

"It's Christmas for us," said Catherine, giving her mother another mighty hug. "We got the best present of all."

"Why is there two of everybody?" asked Simon, noticing the doppelgängers for the very first time. If the concept was difficult for Catherine and Jason to understand, imagine how absurd the whole thing sounded to Simon's six-year-old brain when his father tried to explain it to him. Once he had finished, Simon had only one question, and he directed it to his older self. "When you're eight," he said, "do people still boss you around?"

"They sure do," said Simon. "All the time."

"Darn," said Simon, chomping away on the giant wad of gum. "Nothing to look forward to."

"I have a question too," said Olivia. "Being that there are two of everyone but me, what do we do now?"

No one spoke, but they all seemed to agree that, yes, something had to be done.

CHAPTER 16

If the Cheeseman house were a TV show, it would be rated number one, because it was easily the most watched house in town. In addition to the mysterious blue sports car in the alley and the long black car down the block, two others had recently shown up. The first was a dull gray car sitting on a side street and facing the Cheeseman residence. Inside the car were two dull men in dull gray suits with dull gray hats.

To their mothers the men were known by their birth names, but to each other and to the supersecret government organization for which they worked, where all employees are given initials and those initials are always spelled out, they were known as Aitch Dee and El Kyoo.

"I don't get it," said El Kyoo, whose appetite for sandwiches the size of waffle irons had been responsible for his bottom-heavy, bowling-pin shape. Aitch Dee, on the other hand, was quite broad in the shoulders but very skinny in the legs, causing him to very much resemble a kite.

"You don't get what?" asked the kite-shaped secret agent.

"I don't get why we have to sit here all day and night

and watch this stupid house." El Kyoo took another bite of his giant sandwich, made with six types of cheese, nine different kinds of meat, and no kinds of vegetables.

"I don't want to be here any more than you do," said Aitch Dee. "I'd rather be home organizing my collection of rare and hard-to-find nickels. But do you hear me complaining?"

"Actually, I can't hear much of anything when I'm chewing," said El Kyoo, taking another bite of his double-decker cholesterol sandwich.

While Aitch Dee and El Kyoo were watching the Cheeseman house and talking about nickels and chewing, another car was parked just a block away. This one was small and brown and of unknown make and model. Behind the wheel sat Pavel Dushenko, an international superspy operating on a very limited budget, due to his country's recent economic problems.

He held an old soup can tightly to his ear and listened with great concentration for any conversation originating from the Cheeseman house that might make its way along the string that had been tied to a second tin can, which had been secretly duct-taped to the vent from the kitchen fan. "I hear nothink, Leon," he said in his very thick accent. "But don't worry, my leetle minkey friend. We will all the time very soon get LVR, for which will be very good, and also not bad."

Leon was Pavel's partner in espionage, and he was, indeed, a very talented monkey (or minkey, if you will), with the ability to do impressions of just about any animal, including a very convincing parrot imitating a myna bird mimicking a parakeet imitating a walrus with a Boston accent. Leon showed his excitement for the possibility of obtaining Ethan and Olivia's fabulous LVR by screaming and repeatedly slapping himself on the head in what appeared to be a spot-on impersonation of a monkey who has just been informed that his hair is on fire.

Were his hair on fire, finding water to put it out would not be difficult, because on the backseat of the car sat a ten-gallon aquarium, home to Leon's three beloved goldfish, swimming placidly in and out of the columns of a miniature replica of the Acropolis.

Meanwhile, there was nothing placid about the mood inside the long black car, parked but a hundred feet away. Of all those on the hunt for the LVR, the Plexiwave gang was, by far, the most dangerous and vilest of them all. One of those nasty specimens was listening intently to his cell phone.

"My wife left me a message," said Mr. 88, pulling the phone from his ear. "We're having a Christmas party tonight, and she wants me to pick up a Yule log on the way home."

"So?" said Mr. 207. "What's the problem?"

"The problem is I know what a log is, but what the heck is a yule?"

"I think it's an animal of some kind," said Mr. 29, back from sick leave but still with a runny nose and scratchy throat. Some evil villains love their jobs so much, they insist upon coming to work even when they're sick.

"Yes, I believe you're right," said Mr. 207. "A yule is what you get when you cross a yak with a mule."

"Oh. So then a Yule log is something you definitely wouldn't want to step in," said Mr. 88.

"Exactly," said Mr. 207.

"Quiet!" shouted Mr. 5, a vein the size of a Polish sausage bulging from his right temple. "A Yule log is a log, plain and simple. You put it in the fireplace and set it on fire. Get it?"

The others took a moment to consider this. "Wouldn't that be kind of smelly?" asked Mr. 207.

"It's a log made of wood! There is no animal known as a yule. Now can we just drop it? I can't hear myself think with all your pointless yammering and jabbering."

It was instantly quiet in the car, without the slightest bit of yammering or jabbering, though there was a small amount of sniffling. The vein on Mr. 5's bony head shrank to the size of a gherkin pickle, and he could finally hear himself think. And what he was thinking was this: "I certainly hope Olivia Cheeseman enjoyed her coffee this morning, heh heh heh," and, "I wonder if her husband has a nice suit to wear to the funeral, tee hee hee."

What the internally giggling Mr. 5 did not know was that Olivia had consumed no coffee that morning. And, as far as husbands were concerned, she now had two of them, including one who had traveled from the future to foil Mr. 5's evil plan.

That particular husband was, at that very moment, pacing back and forth in the living room of the house, while the other sat on the couch along with their mutual wife as the three of them joined forces to find a solution to the highly awkward state of affairs in which they now found themselves.

"I'm just not sure what to do," said Ethan the elder to his beloved wife. "Now that the children and I have seen you again, I don't think we could bear to be without you."

"Oh, that's so sweet," said Olivia. Then, turning to the younger Ethan with a devious smile, she remarked, "You never say things like that to me anymore."

Ethan could only stammer and stutter something about being too busy and too wrapped up in his work.

"But," the other Ethan continued, "we can't stay. It just wouldn't work."

"Oh, I don't know," said Olivia. "With two husbands I'm sure I could get one of you to take out the garbage. Works for me."

Both Ethans gave Olivia the same look. It was her natural beauty that had first attracted them to her, but it was her intelligence and wry sense of humor that had caused them to fall in love with her. And though both Ethans loved her with all their hearts, the older Ethan loved her more because, unlike his younger self, he had known life without her. For two years he had lived a hollow, Olivia-less existence, and it's always easier to fully appreciate something once you've been deprived of it.

It then seemed quite unfair that he would have to be the one to leave her behind.

"The whole thing is a rather difficult situation," said the

younger of the two Ethans. "For instance, can we afford to put six kids through college?"

Olivia rolled her eyes and said, "My husband the pragmatist."

"He does make a good point," agreed the equally pragmatic older Ethan.

"Yes," said Olivia. "But think of the money we'd save on clothing with all the hand-me-downs."

As the adults continued to rack their genius brains, searching for a solution to the existing problem of too many Cheesemans in one place at the same time, the three younger Cheeseman children were showing the three older kids around the house they had once called home. Simon was eager for a visit to his old room.

"Wow, my dirt clod collection," he said, admiring the clumps of dirt resembling celebrities that he had lined up on his dresser for display purposes. They were all there, just as he had left them: Abraham Lincoln, John Wayne, that guy with the big nose from that show he wasn't allowed to watch but sometimes did anyway. He picked up the dirt clod resembling Spider-Man. "I found this one behind the Dumpster in back of the school."

"I know," said Simon. "I was there."

"Oh. Right." Simon returned the clump of dried mud to its place on the dresser next to one that looked just like the Blob. He scanned the room and spotted, on the floor in the corner, what had been one of his favorite toys. "My train set!" he gasped.

"You wanna play with it?" asked the younger of the two

Simons, who'd always wished he'd had a brother closer to his age.

"Sure," said Simon, dropping down to the carpet for a closer look. "But I get to be the engineer."

"And I get to be the conductor," said Gravy-Face Roy.

"Then what do I get to be?" asked Simon.

"You get to be the guy who loads the luggage," came the answer. "And cleans the restroom at the station."

Young Simon seemed disappointed, but when he agreed to the proposed terms it became official. For the first time in his eight years of life, Simon finally had someone he could boss around, even if that someone was himself. This suddenly made everything he had been through almost entirely worthwhile.

In Jason's room, Big and the older Jason were busy impressing the younger with their many tales of adventure. Jason sat on the floor, hanging on their every word as they relayed stories of witch hunters, pirates, haunted castles, and a near-death experience at the hands of a hungry T. rex.

"Wow. And I thought our class field trip to the hydro-electric dam was exciting," said Jason the younger, who actually hadn't found the field trip exciting in the least.

"Yeah, that was pretty boring," agreed Jason the elder. "But not nearly as lame as the one to the pencil factory. Remember that?"

It was then that the younger Jason suddenly realized he was in the presence not of an older brother, but of an older and wiser double—one who shared not only his exact DNA, but his entire history, and was privy to everything he'd ever done or said and to every thought that had ever crossed his mind. He had to admit that he found the whole idea of it a bit disconcerting, to say the least.

"I'm glad you guys came from the future to save Mom's life," he said. "But, to be honest, the whole thing is kind of weird."

"Yeah, I guess it is," agreed Jason, though to him it wasn't nearly as bad. There were two years of his life that were his and his alone, whereas every single moment of the younger Jason's existence was common knowledge shared between the two of them.

"Well," said the younger Jason. "I think I'm gonna go . . . do stuff now."

"Oh. Okay," said Jason. By the time the younger Jason had slinked out of the room, the older one could understand what the adults had been talking about. Having everyone together, coexisting in one place along the Time Arc, simply would not work. "We're going to have to leave here," he said to Big. "Which means we're going to have to leave her. We have to leave Mom behind."

Jason stared at the wall, a dull ache rising from his stomach to his chest. Big clasped his hands tightly between her own. "It will work out, somehow," she said. "One way or another. It has to."

Jason was not so sure, and neither was Catherine as she watched her younger self stand before the mirror in her bedroom, engaged in her morning ritual of lovingly brushing her long auburn hair four hundred times with a brush made of imported porcupine quills. She wondered how the young girl would feel to know that a large chunk of that very same hair had been left back in the year 1668.

She debated whether to tell Catherine what she had learned from Sullivan about her future; that she would one day be President Catherine Cheeseman. She decided against it, and instead simply said, "It's okay. Don't worry."

"Don't worry about what?" asked Catherine, setting the brush down on her dresser and turning to face the Catherine of her future.

"About anything. Life has a funny way of working out."

"I do tend to worry a lot." Catherine sat on the bed next to Catherine.

"I know," said Catherine. "Me too."

"Wow, what a coincidence." The two girls shared a laugh, and the younger Catherine said to the other, "I like your hair."

"Thanks. I like yours too."

They sat for a while in silence, eavesdropping on the muffled voices drifting in from the living room.

"They're out there talking about you guys leaving again," said the younger Catherine. "Are you? Are you going to leave again?"

Whereas Jason had found it extremely uncomfortable to have his older double existing in the same time frame as himself, Catherine decided that she rather liked it.

"I guess we have to," said the older Catherine.

Catherine nodded as if she understood, though there was no way to completely comprehend all this crazy time-travel business. "Where will you go?"

Catherine shrugged. "Back to our own time, I guess. As hard as it'll be, we'll just have to find a way to live without Mom."

The younger Catherine's face developed a frown; not an unhappy frown, but a contemplative one. "Wait a minute," she said. "If Mom doesn't die, then when you go back to your own time, won't she be there too?"

The older Catherine turned to her younger self with a blank look that soon transformed into an enormous smile. "That's it," she said. "Catherine Cheeseman, you are a genius."

"I think you mean *we* are a genius."

"Yes, *we* are a genius. And the beauty of it is, it's so simple, even a monkey could understand it."

CHAPTER 17

I don't understand it," said six-year-old Simon, working away on that rubbery, flavorless wad of gum, which spent eight hours every night on the bedpost gathering flavorless dust.

"Neither do I," said the older Simon, chewing on his smaller but equally bland lump of pink goo.

"Me neither," said Gravy-Face Roy, chewing on nothing at all.

The two Catherines had gathered everyone in the living room for the purpose of presenting their theory; one they hoped would hold water or, more importantly, the solution to the problem of not enough Olivias and too many of everyone else.

"It's simple," said the younger Catherine, pacing while she spoke, a behavior she picked up from her father. "Because you guys came back and saved Mom's life, that means she's still alive in the future."

"Yes, go on," said the younger Ethan, leaning forward in his seat on the couch.

"So all we have to do is go back to our own time," said the elder Catherine. "Problem solved."

"But won't there still be two sets of the rest of us?" asked the elder Jason, quite intelligent himself, but no match for his genius sister.

"There can't be two sets of you," said Catherine the younger. "Don't you see? Your future selves can't be there, because they're here."

Suddenly, the two Ethans jumped to their feet at the very same time and blurted out, "She's right!" They began speaking over each other, conveying the same thoughts but in slightly different words, and the whole thing came out as a mangled, garbled mess. Finally, the younger Ethan stopped and deferred to the other out of respect for his elders.

"Please, go ahead," he said.

"Thank you," said Ethan breathlessly. "I believe the Catherines are definitely on to something. By traveling here from the future and changing the course of events, we've created an entirely new time line."

"A parallel universe," Olivia added.

"Exactly. But when we return to the future, those two realities will cease to coexist. They will no longer run parallel but will intersect, joining aspects of each and creating one congruent time line."

For young Simon, who had just learned to tell time on a regular old clock, all this talk about parallel universes and intersecting time lines was making his spiky-haired head hurt. "Does that mean that two years from now Mom will be alive, but we'll be dead?" he asked, nervously chewing as he awaited the answer.

"No," said the older Catherine. "What it means is that Mom will be alive and you will be us."

This seemed to be just the precise amount of information needed to allay Simon's fears without injuring his brain.

"So then all we have to do is go all the way around the Time Arc again until we're two years into the future, and Mom will be there waiting for us?" asked Jason.

"Exactly," said Ethan. "Unless she were to die in some other way between now and then, which will not happen." He directed that last part of his statement at Ethan the younger. "It will not happen because Ethan will make sure it doesn't happen," he said, sounding like a big-time athlete referring to himself in the third person. "In fact, if anything happens to anyone here, I'll come looking for you."

"Hey, easy now," said the younger Ethan. "There's no need for threats."

Ethan exhaled heavily, realizing just how angry he'd been with himself. "I'm sorry," he said. "I guess I blame you—I mean . . . I blame myself for Olivia's death. As a husband and a father, it's my job to protect my family from harm. And I failed."

"But you made it right, Dad," said the younger Catherine, referring to the elder Ethan as *Dad* for the first time. "That's what you always taught us, isn't it? All people make mistakes, but great people make amends."

Ethan smiled. "Sometimes we parents wonder if our kids are listening to anything we say."

"We're listening," said Catherine. "So tell us. What do we do next?"

Even though Olivia's life had been saved for now, she and the entire Cheeseman family were still in great danger by virtue of the LVR's very existence. It was determined that they would have to go underground and remain there until it was safe to resurface.

"This is what I propose we do," said Ethan the elder. "We remove the battery from the LVR and take it with us. You'll have two years to build another one, so that shouldn't be a problem."

"It's quite heavy," said Ethan the younger. "How will you carry it?"

"We're going to take your car as well."

"You're going to take our car?" said Simon the younger. "But what will we use?"

Ethan reached into his pocket and pulled out a handful of antique coins that had been given to him by Captain Jibby back in 1668. "Here," he said, handing the gold and silver pieces over to the younger Ethan. "A collector will probably give you enough for these to buy a good, reliable used car."

"Thanks," said Ethan.

"Wow," said Simon, peering at the smattering of coins resting in his father's open hand. "Is that pirate money?"

"It sure is," said Simon.

"Okay, let's get moving," said Ethan.

"Shouldn't you wait until dark?" asked Catherine. "That way if anyone is watching the house, they won't see you."

"That's just it," said Ethan. "I want them to see us. We're going to strap furniture to the roof of the car and cover it with that blue tarp in the garage. When we drive away, anyone watching the house will think we're leaving with the LVR and will give chase. That will allow you time to get away."

"And how will *you* get away?" asked Olivia.

"We've done it before," said Ethan. "We can do it again."

Olivia and the two Ethans soon learned the value of having six children when all pitched in, along with Big, to carry the couch (or chesterfield, if you prefer), the recliner, two lamps, and the kitchen table to the garage to be strapped to the roof of the family station wagon.

"Remember," said Ethan the elder, when he and the other Ethan had thrown the tarp over the furniture and lashed it to the roof. "Once we're gone, don't waste any time. Get a car, then pack up the LVR and hit the road. Change your names and lie low until the exact date that we first traveled back in time in the LVR, two years from now. If Catherine's theory is correct, Olivia will wake up that morning to find the rest of you gone. And that's when we'll return."

"But if we're to go into hiding, then how will I find you?" asked Olivia.

Ethan took a pen and piece of scrap paper from his workbench and scribbled something down. A genius must always keep multiple scraps of paper handy for whenever inspiration might strike. "Meet us here," he said, handing the paper to Olivia. She took it, and Ethan clutched her by the shoulders. Looking her straight in the eye, he said, "Be extremely careful. Don't trust anyone. Eat plenty of fruits and vegetables, and don't go out in the rain without a hat. And remember to take your vitamins. And always—"

Olivia smiled. "Okay, okay. I'm not a kid, you know."

"I know," said Ethan. "It's just that losing you once was too much to handle. I want to make sure that nothing happens to you again. To any of you. Is that understood? I want you kids to promise me you'll do everything necessary to stay out of danger."

"Don't worry," said Ethan the younger. "They're a smart bunch."

"You have no idea," said Ethan the elder. He sized up the younger children, then the older. "They're more than just smart. These kids have the hearts of heroes. You'll see."

Ethan gave Olivia one last kiss, which lasted only until his three children muscled him out of the way, hugging their mother as if they might never see her again. And, if Catherine's theory proved incorrect in any way, they very well might not. For that reason, they were afraid to let her go, but there was no other way, and they knew what had to be done. One by one, they peeled themselves away and said their good-byes to their younger selves.

"Try not to worry so much," said the younger Catherine to the elder.

"Thanks," said Catherine with a smile. "You too. And keep practicing your archery. I happen to know it will come in handy someday."

Young Jason offered his hand to his older counterpart.

"It was very nice meeting you," he said. "And I'm going to do my best to make you proud of me."

"You'll do great," said Jason.

"Thanks for letting me be the engineer," said Simon to Simon. "Sorry I was so bossy."

"It's okay," said Simon. "I'm kind of used to it." Both Simons blew a large pink bubble at the same time. The younger Simon's bubble popped first, which allowed him to be the first to say, "Jinx."

"It doesn't count with bubbles," said Simon. Then, suddenly realizing he was being bossy again, he said, "I mean, good one. You got me."

Ethan gave his younger self a parting handshake before he and his three children, Big, Digs, and Pinky piled into the old family station wagon and buckled up for what very well could be a harrowing ride.

"We'll see you in a couple of years," said young Jason.

"We'll *be* you in a couple of years," Catherine the younger corrected.

"Actually, for us it should be a matter of just a few days," said the older Ethan. That's how long he anticipated it would take to get back to the LVR, replace the battery, and make the trip around the Time Arc to two years into the future. His level of optimism was high. For one thing, this time they wouldn't have to worry about being bumped off the Time Arc when passing the Great Sync. They could thank Signor Gioachino Rossini for this. Because of him and his *William Tell Overture*, they now had the formula for the proper angle of trajectory.

Ethan started the engine and activated the automatic garage door opener. The younger Cheesemans and their parents watched as the station wagon inched out of the garage and into the driveway. The car stopped, and the garage door came down behind it. A second later, they heard the sharp squealing of tires.

CHAPTER 18

I know what gold is," said Mr. 88 while biting the nails of his large ringed fingers and spitting them out the open window of the long black sedan. "But what the heck are frankincense and myrrh?"

"Frankincense sounds like some kind of aftershave to me," said Mr. 29, followed by a long sniff of his runny nose.

"I think you're right," Mr. 207 concurred. "Frankincense is aftershave that smells like frankfurters. And myrrh, I believe, is an abbreviation for monkey fur."

"Monkey fur?" snapped Mr. 5. "The Three Wise Men brought gifts of gold, monkey fur, and aftershave that smells like hot dogs? Seriously, what is wrong with you people? And roll that window up, it's freezing in here."

"If I roll up the window, then what will I do with my fingernails?" said Mr. 88.

"I don't know, try keeping them on your fingers."

Mr. 88 looked at his right hand, with two fingernails that still had yet to be bitten. He sighed and rolled his window up just as Mr. 5's cell phone rang. Mr. 5 removed the matchbook-sized device from the pocket of his suit jacket. "Quiet everyone, it's headquarters," he said. "It's probably Mr. 1 calling to congratulate me on a job well done. Hello, Mr. 5 here."

Mr. 5's face dropped when he heard the voice at the other end of the phone. It was a voice that did not belong to Mr. 1.

"Yes, this is Ms. 4," said the woman, whose position with the company Mr. 5 coveted like no other. "I trust you have carried out your mission successfully."

"Yes," said Mr. 5 with a manufactured pleasantness that was barely able to slip through his tightly clenched teeth. "We heard breaking glass a couple of hours ago, most likely Mrs. Cheeseman dropping her empty coffee mug after clutching her chest and collapsing to the floor. We expect the ambulance or, better yet, the hearse to arrive at any moment."

"Good," said Ms. 4. "Because I would hate to be in your shoes should you mess up this time."

"Don't worry," Mr. 5 assured her. "I've got it all under control."

"I certainly hope so," said Ms. 4. "I shall await the official word of Olivia Cheeseman's passing. Good day."

"Same to you," said Mr. 5. "And tell Mr. 1 I said . . . hello? Hello?" Mr. 5 stuffed the cell phone back into his pocket. "She hung up, that wretched old battle-ax. I hate her more than I hate anyone in this car, and believe me, that's saying a lot."

Before the insult could fully sink in, the Cheesemans' garage door opened and the old station wagon crept out onto the driveway, loaded high with something or some things concealed beneath a bright blue tarp.

"Look," shouted Mr. 207. "It's the Cheesemans. They're leaving, and they're taking the LVR."

"Perfect," said Mr. 88, rubbing his giant hands together. "Once they leave their house, anything we do to them is perfectly legal."

"Actually, I don't think it works that way," said Mr. 207.

"Are you calling me a liar?"

"He's calling you an idiot," barked Mr. 5. "Now shut up and follow them."

The station wagon's rear tires let out an ear-piercing chirp, and the car lurched forward out of the driveway and onto the street. Mr. 88 wasted no time starting up the long black car's engine and taking off after the Cheesemans. He was paying far too much attention to the loaded-down station wagon to notice that his was not the only car in pursuit of it.

As the old station wagon took a sharp turn, there were three cars hot on its trail. One car carried a man with gold rings covering each of his fingers. The second car had a glove box that smelled very much like frankfurter cologne, and the third was occupied by an international superspy, whose sidekick just happened to be covered entirely in monkey fur or, for short, myrrh. But no one in any of these cars could be considered terribly wise by any stretch of the imagination, and none of them had any intention of giving the Cheesemans a gift. They were there for one reason and one reason only: to take.

And, as if being followed by three cars full of greedy evildoers wasn't enough for one family to endure, a fourth vehicle, that mysterious blue sports car from the back alley, pulled in behind Pavel and Leon and joined the chase.

"Could you put the sandwich down for one minute?" said Aitch Dee, his knuckles pale white on the wheel as he pulled up behind Mr. 5's black sedan. "I need you to keep your eyes on that station wagon in case I lose it."

"Why can't I can keep my eyes on the car and my mouth on the sandwich at the same time?" whined El Kyoo.

"Just put it away, would you?"

Like Romeo bidding a sad farewell to Juliet, El Kyoo lowered the three pounds of sandwich that still remained outside his bowling-pin-shaped body. He seemed to whimper slightly as he wrapped it in a napkin and placed it lovingly in the glove box, which had never been used to hold gloves, but was a frequent home to El Kyoo's excessively large lunches.

The station wagon squealed around a sharp corner and down Musgrave Street, startling the Baldersons' vicious fourteen-year-old schnauzer. The black sedan followed closely with the dull gray car carrying the dull gray men pulling up close behind it.

"We've got to get to them before Plexiwave does," said Aitch Dee.

"Or that little weasel Pavel Dushenko," said El Kyoo.

"Pavel Dushenko? That moron? Trust me, he's got no idea the LVR even exists."

Contrary to the opinion of Agent Aitch Dee, Pavel Dushenko and his loyal sidekick, Leon, knew very well of the LVR's existence, and of the importance of taking it.

The little brown car rounded the corner with the others, causing Leon's fish to slosh about in their tank like three mismatched socks in a washing machine on full swirl. Leon voiced his displeasure by screaming and slapping himself on the head, a gesture Pavel mistook for a childlike enthusiasm.

"Yes, Leon," shouted Pavel over the racing of the little car's overworked engine. "I agree. Getting LVR will be very happy thing to do, and also not sad."

"They're right behind us," said Catherine, checking the side view mirror from her position in the front passenger seat. The best thing about her brother having a girlfriend was that she got to sit up front for a change, because, of course, Jason just couldn't bear to be more than three feet away from Big at any time. In fact, it must have been true love, because not only did Jason volunteer to sit in the backseat, he offered to sit in the middle, on the dreaded hump.

"This is just what I hoped would happen," said Ethan. "The farther we can lure them from the house, the longer the others will have to get away. Hold on!"

Ethan turned the wheel with such force that the station wagon nearly rolled onto its side as it skidded around a corner, heading for the highway out of town.

For the Cheesemans the ride was frightening and

intense, but for Big it was her first opportunity to see the twenty-first century in daylight hours, and everything was downright fascinating.

"The future is a very different place," she said, mesmerized as they passed logging trucks hauling enormous, branchless trees, superstores the size of the entire settlement of Shattuckton, and a man dressed as an ice-cream cone standing on the corner and waving at passing cars.

Simon waved back. "Hey Dad, can we stop for ice cream?"

"I want bubble-gum ice cream," said Gravy-Face Roy.

"Sorry, guys," said Ethan. "When we get to where we're going, you can have as much ice cream as you like. Right now, though, we can't stop for anything."

But as they veered onto the highway, it became apparent that they might have no choice but to stop when a red light on the dashboard popped on, informing Ethan that the station wagon was low on gas.

"Darn it," he said, his fist meeting the steering wheel with a sharp thwack. "In all the excitement I didn't even think to check the fuel level." Ethan looked in the rearview mirror to confirm that the parade of cars was still there. "I think it's time we lightened our load, if you know what I mean."

Cutting the ropes that held the furniture to the roof would be a very simple task were the car parked in the driveway and not careening down the freeway at eighty-five miles per hour. "Jason, can you do it?" asked Ethan.

"I can do it," Jason confirmed.

"Good. Now take Big's hunting knife and cut the ropes."

"No," said Big. "I'll do it." She unbuckled her seat belt and removed her hunting knife from its scabbard.

"Hand me that knife," said Jason. "It's too dangerous."

"It's no more dangerous for me than it is for you." Big looked at the window with no idea how to open it. "Please," she said.

"Okay," Jason relented. "But be careful." He lowered the automatic window and held tightly to Big's ankles as the girl leaned out of the speeding car, the wind tossing her braids violently about. In a matter of seconds, her blue baseball cap was ripped from her head and sent bouncing along the road.

"Look!" shouted Mr. 207. "There's a kid climbing out of the car."

"She's got a knife," screamed Mr. 29. "Get down!"

"Get down?" scoffed Mr. 5. "It's a knife, not a hand grenade. What harm could a knife do?"

With the razor-sharp implement, Big sliced through the rope that held the tarp to the roof. Once untethered, the tarp took to the air like a large blue kite. Its flight was short-lived, and it quickly came to rest on the windshield of the long black car.

"I can't see!" yelled Mr. 88 as the black sedan raced blindly down the highway.

"Then pull over!" ordered Mr. 5.

Horns honked and tires screeched as Mr. 88 spun the wheel to the right, crossed two lanes of traffic, and drove over the shoulder, off the road, and directly toward a shopping complex. The blue tarp took to the air once more just in time for Mr. 88 and his fellow Misters to see that they were only seconds from crashing into a supermarket. Suddenly, the car was filled with a four-part harmony of terrified screams.

"Aaahhh!"

"Yiiiieeee!"

"Nooooo!"

"Whaaaaa!"

Mr. 88 stiffened his leg against the brake pedal, and the car went into a wild skid. A horrified shopper abandoned her cart just as the car slammed into it, sending the cart, and her hard-earned purchases, high into the air.

The car jerked to a halt, and a full ten seconds passed before it was showered with falling groceries, including: several cans of soup, a dozen eggs, a gallon of bubble-gum ice cream, and a very large chunk of wood, which smashed through the windshield and landed, amid a shower of broken glass, directly in Mr. 5's lap.

"This," said Mr. 5, when the barrage was over, "is a Yule log."

While the blue tarp had gotten rid of one of the pursuers, three still remained. And now they all knew the Cheesemans weren't carrying the LVR, but a bunch of old furniture. Well, most of them knew.

"That's the darndest-looking time machine I've ever seen," said El Kyoo. "It looks like a bunch of furniture."

"That's because it *is* a bunch of furniture," said Aitch Dee.

"Well," said El Kyoo, "if I had known it was that easy to make a time machine, I would've built one myself."

Big sliced through the rope holding the couch to the roof rack, but it failed to budge. She tried reaching up and shoving it, but the couch was just too heavy.

"It refuses to fall!" shouted Big.

"Okay," said Ethan. "Hang on!"

Many of our nation's highways and byways are equipped with a handy little feature known as a rumble strip—raised bumps at the edge of a lane designed to alert drivers that they have drifted too far to one side. This was one of those highways. Ethan veered over until the tires on the left side of the car came in contact with the strips. At eighty-five miles per hour, they created quite a vibration; certainly enough to cause the couch to begin inching its way toward the edge of the roof.

"Look out!" yelled El Kyoo when the couch slipped off the back of the station wagon and onto the road directly in front of the dull gray car. The car slammed into the couch and drove up onto it, leaving its front wheels off the ground but its rear wheels still in contact with the road.

The back of the car spun around and crossed the centerline. It narrowly missed being T-boned by an eighteen-wheeler full of cymbals, xylophones, and banjos. It jumped the shoulder, screamed through a parking lot, and smashed through the window of a sandwich shop, sending traumatized patrons running for cover and finally coming to a stop directly in front of the counter.

"Wow," said Aitch Dee, trying to catch his breath, his fingers fused to the steering wheel. "Unbelievable."

"No kidding," said El Kyoo. "Eight bucks for a meatball sandwich? Ridiculous."

As Aitch Dee waited for his fingers to unclench and El Kyoo waited for the price of meatball sandwiches to come down, Ethan Cheeseman and his passengers were celebrating like a submarine crew that has just scored a direct hit on an aircraft carrier. "Nice shot, Big," yelled Catherine.

But Big couldn't hear a thing with the wind thundering past her eardrums. And besides, she was just getting started. Jason struggled to keep hold of her as she gripped the roof rack and inched out farther. If she were to slip and fall at this point, there wasn't much Jason could do to save her. She sliced through the rope holding the recliner.

"Leon, I am big worry," said Pavel. "I don't see LVR. Only big, comfortable chair."

Pavel's myrrh-covered sidekick responded by screaming and jumping up and down on the backseat in an effort to correct Pavel, for it was not just a big, comfortable chair, but a big, comfortable *flying* chair, and it was flying right toward the little brown car.

The chair hit the asphalt and splintered into pieces as Pavel swerved just in time to miss the bulk of it.

"Ha ha!" he yelled. "You are not so easy to have rid of the great Pavel Dushenko!"

He turned to high-five Leon and, in doing so, failed to see a living-room lamp roll off the roof rack and smash through his car's windshield. Then the lamp, perhaps deciding it rather enjoyed breaking glass, continued into the backseat, where it struck the fish tank and shattered it into hundreds of tiny pieces.

Leon gripped his head tightly at the temples and let out a primal scream as his beloved fish flopped about helplessly on the backseat. He motioned for Pavel to pull over, doing everything in his power to impress upon him the need for water, but Pavel's and Leon's priorities were, at that moment, not exactly in sync.

"No, Leon. If we stop for water, we will fail, and also not succeed. Your feeshes must make ultimate sacrifice for good of country."

Leon scooped up the feeshes, held them lovingly in his hands, and prepared to say good-bye.

Just then the kitchen table flew off the station wagon, landing directly beneath the little brown car. As the car dragged it along the pavement at ninety miles per hour, sparks began to shoot up from the road. Leon sniffed and made a face.

"That was not me," said Pavel.

The burning smell grew in intensity until finally, with an enormous bang, the hood flew off the car and flames shot up from the engine six feet into the air and blew back in through the missing windshield. The flames danced perilously close to Pavel's petrified face. As he let go of the wheel to try to fend off the fire, the flaming brown car swerved out of control, flying off the side of the road, through a chain-link fence, across a city park, and into a pond.

With a sharp hiss the car hit the water, instantly

dousing the flames. Then, as Leon breathed a sigh of relief, the car slowly began to sink until pond water poured in through the empty space where the windshield once resided. Leon rejoiced. He lowered his goldfish into the cold, slimy water and watched happily as they swam about the backseat of the car. He then watched somewhat less happily as the fish swam out through the broken windshield and into the pond, where they lived happily ever after, until two days later when they were eaten by ducks.

With Pavel and Leon sitting up to their necks in slimy pond water and lamenting their failure to get the LVR, Big dropped back into the station wagon and placed her knife into its scabbard.

"Great job," said Jason, bursting with pride.

"Now that was fun," said Big, who had never smiled quite so broadly.

She had single-handedly gotten rid of three of the four cars, but one persistent pest remained, and the Cheesemans' four-wheeled submarine was all out of torpedoes.

"There's still one car following us," said Jason.

"Who is it?" asked Simon.

The mysterious blue sedan kept its distance, which, along with its tinted windshield, made it impossible to get a good look at the driver. "I don't know," said Jason.

"We've got to lose it somehow," said Ethan. "We're almost out of gas." He took another look at the fuel gauge. There was a service station up ahead on the right, but he didn't dare pull over now. He increased his speed, pushing the rattly old station wagon to its very limits, but the blue car stayed right with them. He passed another gas station. The needle on the fuel gauge had long ago stopped moving, having dropped as far as it could go.

Ethan knew he had one shot at losing the mysterious blue car and one shot only. He looked ahead and saw they were about to enter a long, dark tunnel. A sign at the entrance advised motorists to make sure their headlights were on. Ethan ignored the sign. He sped up to widen his lead on the blue car before entering the tunnel.

He took a deep breath, gripped the wheel tightly, and hoped what he was about to attempt would not be the last thing he would ever do. Pinky sensed something was up and let out her patented portent of doom, a low, steady growl.

The station wagon was halfway through the tunnel before Ethan got up the nerve to make his move. "Hold on," he said. Then he hit the brakes and spun the wheel hard to the left, sending the car into a violent spin. The children's screams perfectly complemented the screeching tires. When the station wagon finally came to a rest, it was facing in the exact opposite direction.

Seconds later, the blue car flew by, and Ethan gunned the engine, driving through the tunnel directly toward oncoming traffic.

"Dad, look out!" shouted Catherine.

Horns blared as Ethan swerved right, then left, then right again, narrowly avoiding several head-on collisions.

The moment he cleared the tunnel he swerved off the road, across the center divider, and back onto the highway, where he continued to drive back the way they had come.

"Sorry about that, everybody," said Ethan.

His passengers were far too traumatized to speak as he pulled off the road and into a gas station just as the car's engine sputtered and died. He coasted the final thirty feet to the pump, then slumped forward, resting his forehead on the steering wheel. "We made it," he said.

"We sure did, Dad," said Jason. "Great driving."

"Thanks," said Ethan. "Now all we have to do is travel twelve hundred miles and hope that the LVR is still there, and that Catherine's theory is more than just a theory."

ADVICE FOR MOTORISTS

Driving a car can be a very dangerous business. Believe me, I know what I'm talking about, because I was once involved in a hit-and-run accident, and let me just say, it's a good thing I got the heck out of there.

One way to help avoid mishaps on the road is to be sure to keep your car's equipment in proper working order. Just last week I found myself driving behind a very inconsiderate motorist whose car had no brake lights, if you can believe such a thing. This angered me to the point that I considered honking at him, until I recalled that my horn has been broken for years. And, as I would discover, honking at someone without the use of a horn will get you some very strange looks indeed, particularly from any nearby geese.

Another perilous aspect to the driving experience is road rage, of which I have been a victim on several occasions. One such incident began when someone thought it would be humorous to sneak over to my house and write the words *Wash me* with his finger on my car's dust-caked surface.

Thanks to this incompetent criminal leaving both his fingerprints and a handwriting sample at the scene, I was able to determine that it was my cousin, Gilbert Soup, and I did not find his little joke the least bit funny, though I did think it quite hysterical when I sneaked over to his house and wrote on his car. With a nail. *Paint me.*

This harmless little prank resulted in a serious case of road rage as I ran down the road, just steps ahead of my raging cousin, then got into my dusty car and sped away.

And though I would always advise you to drive your car with the utmost caution, sometimes it is absolutely necessary to go as fast as you can, throwing caution to the wind and furniture off the roof.

CHAPTER 19

Twelve hours into their journey back to where they had left the LVR, the children, the animals, and Gravy-Face Roy slept while Ethan fought the urge to join them. After all they'd been through, to have it all end by falling asleep at the wheel and driving off the road would be tragic beyond belief. Ethan shook his head and slapped himself in the face. He cracked the window, hoping some cold air might help snap him out of his stupor.

The sound of the night air rushing in caused Jason to stir. "Dad?" he said. "You want me to drive for a while?"

Long ago, when Ethan and his children first went on the run, he made the decision to teach Jason how to operate a motor vehicle so that if anything were to happen to him, there would be someone who could drive the rest of the family to safety.

"I think I'll be okay," said Ethan. "I could use someone to talk to, though."

"Sure," said Jason. He sat up and leaned forward, resting

his arms across the back of the front passenger seat. "What do you want to talk about?"

"Oh, nothing in particular," said Ethan unconvincingly. "Just a little small talk to help me stay awake."

"Oh, okay. Who do you think's gonna win the Super Bowl this year?"

"I'm very worried," said Ethan.

"You shouldn't be," said Jason. "This is the past, remember? We already know who won the Super Bowl."

"Too bad we don't have any money to bet." Ethan smiled and chuckled, but the smile quickly disappeared. "No, I'm worried about us. About what's going to happen when we get back to the LVR. It's all been one disaster after another. Why should this time be any different?"

"Because it will be," said Jason. "Because it has to be."

"How can you be so sure?"

"I'm not. I was just trying to make you feel better. But the truth is, I'm worried too."

With neither of them wanting to think about all the things that might go horribly wrong in their upcoming trip around the Time Arc, the conversation once again turned to football and other things of little importance. Ethan and his similarly worried son continued to talk until the sun came up, which caused the rest of his passengers to stir.

"Are we there yet?" groaned Simon, just before realizing his bubble gum had fallen from his mouth and was now stuck to Gravy-Face Roy, who was stuck to the backseat.

"A few hours yet," said Ethan. "There's a town coming up. We'll stop and stretch our legs and get some breakfast."

Simon had managed to separate his sock puppet from the backseat by the time the station wagon pulled off the highway and cruised into the parking lot of a roadside diner called Ruth's Country Kitchen. He parked around back, keeping the car out of view from the road. They let the animals out to do their business, and by that I do not mean that the animals engaged in the buying and selling of dog biscuits. Once their transactions were completed, the animals were returned to the car and the humans entered the restaurant, where the menu featured a "Bottomless Cup of Coffee," "All-You-Can-Eat Pancakes," and an "Endless Salad Bar," which included a warning to patrons to be careful not to fall off the edge of the earth.

The hostess, a stout woman in a brown polyester uniform, escorted them to a booth by the window looking onto the highway. They ate as though they hadn't eaten in days, and Ethan drank coffee as if he hadn't slept in weeks.

They ordered a side of bacon and sausage for Pinky and Digs, and when it arrived, Ethan paid the bill and they headed for the exit. No sooner had they stepped out of the restaurant and into the parking lot than Ethan yelled, "Get down!"

He ducked behind a parked car, and the children did likewise.

"What? What is it?" asked Catherine.

Ethan rose up slowly to see the blue sports car racing down the highway. "I thought we lost them," he said.

"Are you sure that's the same car?" asked Jason, who was pretty sure it was the same car.

"I don't know," said Ethan. "It sure looked like it. Then again, maybe I'm just being paranoid."

They climbed back into the car. With four hours of driving still ahead of them, Ethan was, nevertheless, reluctant to leave the parking lot. He drove slowly out from behind the restaurant, his eyes darting back and forth with a paranoia fueled by too much coffee, too little sleep, and too many people chasing him.

He eased out onto the highway and saw no sign of the blue sports car; nor did it appear at any time over the next two hundred and twenty miles.

"It looks like we're getting close," said Catherine, when they drove past the airport they had recently broken into with the help of yours truly.

"We are," said Ethan. "We just have one more stop to make." He guided the station wagon off the highway, past a hay field and a rutabaga farm, then down a rural road, past a familiar-looking mailbox, and up a long drive to a luxurious mansion rising majestically above its impeccably landscaped grounds.

"Wait here. I'll be right back." The children watched as Ethan hurried from the car to the mansion's oversized front door. He rang the bell and waited. And waited. Finally, the door swung open to reveal a small, elderly woman wearing a housecoat, her tiny face encumbered with large, thick glasses. Encircling the back of her right ear was a hearing aid the size of a croissant. The woman was Roberta Soup, or, as she was known to some of us, Mom.

"Hello, you must be Mrs. Soup," Ethan began. "I'm looking for Professor Acorn Boxley."

The woman turned and hollered back into the house. "Filbert! There's a fella here selling boxes of acorns!"

"We'll take two!" came the voice of the woman's husband from somewhere deep inside the mansion.

"No, no, I'm not selling acorns," said Ethan.

"He's not selling acorns!" yelled Roberta.

"Then forget it!" hollered Filbert.

"I'm Ethan Cheeseman," said Ethan. "I went to school with your son, Cuthbert."

"Oh." Once again the woman turned and yelled down the hallway. "Cuthbert! One of your little school friends is here!"

An awkward sixty seconds of silence passed before Professor Boxley showed up at the door. "Cuthbert. There you are," said Roberta. "Put on a jacket if you're going to be playing outside."

"I'm not Cuthbert, Mrs. Soup," said the professor, his patience obviously at its breaking point. "I thank you kindly for your hospitality, but, as I told you before, my name is Acorn Boxley."

"Filbert! There's a fella here selling boxes of acorns!"

"We'll take two!"

As Ethan bid Mrs. Soup good day and rushed the professor back to the awaiting car, the old man was full of gratitude for being rescued and of Roberta's patented Spam® chowder, having eaten two and a half bowls for lunch.

"Well?" he asked with a small, chowdery burp. "How did it go? With Olivia?"

Ethan opened the driver's-side door and looked at the professor over the roof of the car. "She's alive," he said. "She's alive and well."

The professor smiled and nodded. "Well done, Ethan. Well done."

Simon made room for the professor by climbing over the backseat and into the area of a station wagon officially known as the *way back*, so dubbed because it is the area at the very back of the car. Professor Boxley squeezed into the regular backseat, buckled up, and off they went. It was only a couple of minutes by car. Ethan got as close as he could to the site before the road came to an end.

"It's right over that hill," he said.

Everyone scrambled out of the car, just happy not to be sitting for a change, even though they were gearing up for a very long ride around the Time Arc. Though their destination was but two years into the future, Ethan had discovered that the Time Arc was a one-way street, and the only way to get two years into the future was to travel all the way back, several billion years, to the beginning of time, then over the Great Sync to the end of time, and then continue backward. It would be a bit like going from North Dakota to South Dakota by flying over the North Pole and all the way around the earth. Not practical, but it's not as though they had another option.

Ethan opened the tailgate, helped Simon out of the way

back, and then pulled out the large replacement battery. "Okay, let's go."

They started toward the LVR, but the sudden sound of a car's engine stopped them in their tracks. They turned to see the blue sports car thundering down the road.

"Uh-oh. What do we do, Dad?" asked Catherine.

"We run," said Jason.

"No," said Ethan. "Not this time."

The car approached quickly and came to a stop some twenty feet from the white station wagon. For a moment, nothing happened. Ethan and the others stared at the car, and the car stared back. Big placed her hand on the handle of her knife. Then, the driver's-side door opened and out stepped a pretty woman in a dark blue business suit. She had short blond hair and sharp features.

"Ethan Cheeseman?" she shouted across the distance that separated them.

"Stay away from my family," Ethan commanded.

It was obvious the woman thought little of Ethan's directive as she began walking right toward him.

"I'm warning you," said Ethan. "You'll never get the LVR without a fight. So if you don't want to get hurt, you'll get back into your car, drive back to Plexiwave, and tell your bosses to leave us alone."

The woman continued walking. "Plexiwave?" she said. "There must be some confusion here. I don't work for Plexiwave." Suddenly, she reached beneath her jacket. Ethan took a step back. Big tightened her grip on the knife handle, then relaxed it again when the woman pulled out . . . a card. A business card, by the looks of it. She walked up casually and handed the card to Ethan.

"You're a hard man to find, Mr. Cheeseman." She reached out her hand and Ethan took it, tentatively. "My name is Leona Stubblefield. I work for Horace Mortensen."

"Horace Mortensen?" said Jason. "*The* Horace Mortensen?"

"Who's Horace Mortensen?" asked Ethan.

"He's the head of Central Studios," said Professor Boxley, a huge movie buff who knew all there was to know about the film business.

"That's right," said Leona. "He sent me to find you. Central Studios is prepared to pay you a handsome sum for the movie rights to your rather inspiring story."

Ethan chuckled, and his chuckle soon turned into an all-out laugh. "That's it?" he said. "That's all you want with us?"

"That's all," said Leona. "To help you with your decision, I've written an amount on the back."

Ethan flipped the card over and his eyes widened at the figure scrawled upon it in ballpoint pen. "Wow. And how exactly did you find out about our story?"

"It's what I'm paid to do," Leona said. "So what do you say? Can I call my boss and tell him the good news?"

"Hey, Dad," said Simon. "Are we gonna be in a movie?"

"No," said Ethan. He handed the card back to Leona. "Thanks, Ms. Stubblefield. I appreciate your interest, but we're pretty private people."

"Keep it," said Leona of the card. "You might change your mind."

"Maybe," said Ethan. "I guess you never know what the future holds." He slid the card into his shirt pocket with the knowledge that he *did* know a little bit about what the future held. "In the meantime, if you don't mind, we've got a bit of family business to tend to."

"I understand," said Leona. "I look forward to one day hearing from you. Good luck."

"Thanks," said Ethan. "We'll need it."

As suddenly as she had arrived, the woman walked back to her blue sports car, climbed in, and drove off in a cloud of dust.

ADVICE ON SUCCEEDING IN HOLLYWOOD

It's been said that Hollywood is the stuff dreams are made of: nine-foot-tall armadillos with two heads, four sideburns, and Irish accents who chase you around waving rusty can openers until you wake up sobbing and clutching your stuffed bunny.

Hmm. Perhaps I'm sharing too much. One day I must invest in a computer with a delete button. Anyway, back to Hollywood.

Each year, thousands of people from all over the world set out for Hollywood in search of fame and fortune. Most of them never find it, even though it is clearly marked on the map. Still, of those who do manage to get there, only a very small percentage will find parking. And of those few, only a handful will attain the stardom they so desire.

Personally, I have never had the urge to seek fame and, in fact, have done a very good job keeping myself out of the spotlight, except for a single, unauthorized appearance on a website called WhenGerbilsAttack .com.

But, for those who do crave the glow of the limelight, what is the best way to differentiate oneself from the masses and become a household name? One way is by changing your name to Drano or Butter-Flavored Pam.

Another less conventional way is through hard work, which will include hours and hours of acting lessons, during which time you will learn the fine art of how to make believe. Then again, you could always cut out the middleman and simply make believe you are taking acting lessons. This will save time and precious money that could be better spent on important things like plastic surgery, hair dye, fake teeth, and wrinkle creams designed to give you very creamy wrinkles.

But the most reliable and time-tested way to succeed in Hollywood is to make sure you are in the right place at the right time, or, in the case of the Cheesemans, the right places at the right times.

CHAPTER 20

Everyone knows that time flies, though, oddly enough, it does not float. This illustrates just how unpredictable time can be, which is precisely why Ethan was so concerned about the journey on which he and his family were about to embark. Each trip around the Time Arc held the potential for disaster or, at the very least, disappointment.

The good news was that they found the LVR exactly where they'd left it, just across the way from Soup Manor, sitting in the middle of a wide expanse of cactus and sagebrush. Or is it cacti and sagebrushes? Or cacti and sagebri?

Either way, the point is that, so far, all was going according to plan, which is something to which the Cheesemans had not become accustomed. Ethan replaced the old battery with the one he'd borrowed from his younger self, then took a quick walk around the LVR, performing a visual inspection.

"Looks good," he said. "Well, gang, I guess this is it."

"I guess so," said Catherine, who perhaps felt more

pressure than any of them, given that it was her theory on which they were placing their highest hopes.

"No matter what happens," said Ethan, "we're still a family, and that's one thing that will never change. Now, before we go, does anyone have any questions?"

"Yes," said Simon, raising his non–sock puppet hand. "Why can't we be in a movie?"

Ethan smiled and scruffed up Simon's hair. "Because we've got more important things to think about right now, that's why." Then he clapped his hands together as if breaking a huddle and said, "Okay, let's do it."

They all climbed into the LVR and took their places: Ethan and Professor Boxley at the controls, Catherine and Simon seated right behind them, the animals curled up beneath their seats, and Jason and Big sitting in the third row, which technically was the LVR's way back.

Ethan hit the switch, and the LVR's thrusters fired up. He and the professor barked out commands and several series of numbers to each other while simultaneously flicking switches and turning knobs.

Simon gripped Catherine's hand tightly, Jason latched on to Big's, and Gravy-Face Roy chewed nervously on the seat cushion.

Ethan looked to the professor, who nodded that all systems were go. Destination: the exact day they had first traveled back into the past, two years, six months, and eleven days from now. Ethan threw the switch, and off they went.

As they raced backward through time, the chronometer raced with them. Professor Boxley periodically shouted out dates to keep Ethan informed as to their position in time. "Thirteen forty-two. Two hundred thousand BCE. One point two billion." An hour passed, then two as the LVR raced along, vibrating steadily like a car driving across rumble strips. The noise was prohibitive to conversation, not that anyone had anything worthwhile to say, and even if they did, it would be difficult for words to make their way past the lumps in their throats.

"Approaching the Great Sync," yelled Professor Boxley.

"Okay," Ethan hollered back. "This is it!"

With a sharp jolt and slight yaw to the left, the LVR passed the Great Sync, coming out on the other side, at the very end of time.

"We made it!" the professor cheered.

"Not yet we haven't," said Ethan, knowing full well they'd only won half the battle. They still had to land on the exact day in late June when they first disappeared. They would have to stick the landing like an Olympic gymnast. Anything less than a perfect ten would be considered failure.

Once again the professor began counting down the dates. "Three point six billion AD. One point nine billion. Four hundred eighteen thousand."

Another nail-biting hour passed, and by then they were getting close. The numbers raced by so quickly on the chronometer now that Professor Boxley could not keep up with them. It was like trying to read a book while flipping through the pages.

Then, without warning, the LVR stopped. There was no explosion or collision or terrible racket. In fact, there was nothing but silence. Ethan looked at Professor Boxley, and Professor Boxley looked at the chronometer.

"Well?" said Ethan, afraid of what information that tiny little dial might hold.

"June twenty-third," said the professor with a slowly growing smile.

"And we've got the right year?" asked Ethan hopefully.

"We've got the right year," said Professor Boxley.

In his excitement, Ethan tried to jump for joy, but forgot that his seat belt was still fastened. He unbuckled the belt and tried again. The children and Professor Boxley did likewise, laughing, hugging, high-fiving, and celebrating as much as the cramped interior of the LVR would allow. "I knew we'd make it," said Catherine.

"Yes," said Ethan. "We made it to the correct date. Now let's see about the location." His remark was meant to remind everyone that it is always dangerous to declare mission accomplished prematurely. After all, getting there was the easy part. They stuck the landing, but would they go home with the gold?

Ethan looked at the pod door. It almost seemed preferable to remain inside, to wallow in ignorance rather than to face disappointment again. He unlatched the door and pushed it outward. A stream of early summer sunshine greeted their faces as they stepped out into a field of golden spring wheat. Pinky and Digs immediately celebrated their release from the constricted space of the LVR by frolicking, chasing, and rolling about.

"Where are we?" asked Simon.

"Sure smells like North Dakota to me," said Professor Boxley. He closed his eyes and inhaled deeply. Memories rushed in through his nostrils, directly to his brain.

"That's because it is North Dakota," said Ethan.

"Are we supposed to be in North Dakota?" asked Jason.

"We sure are. Come on."

"It reminds me of Shattuckton," said Big, brushing her hand across the tall stalks as Ethan led the group through the field toward the growing sounds of traffic. Where the wheat stopped abruptly, there was a road and several dozen buildings.

"What's that?" asked Catherine.

"That," said Ethan, "is Southwestern North Dakota State University."

"Where you first met Mom," said Jason.

"Exactly."

It was summer session and the place was practically a ghost town, with only a few students walking about.

"I haven't been back here since I retired," said Professor Boxley.

"I haven't been back here since I graduated," said Ethan. "Seems so much smaller now."

He and the others hurried across the road and walked through campus, past the library, the science building, and Melvin Stadium, home of the SWNDSU Fighting Paper Clips. The arena was named after Cyrus Melvin, a wealthy alumnus who had donated the money for the stadium from the enormous fortune he had amassed by inventing the trapdoor on the bottom of the toaster that helps get rid of the crumbs.

"Is that where you played football, Dad?" asked Jason.

"That's where the team played," said Ethan. "I wasn't very good, so my playing time was somewhat limited."

"Nonsense," said Professor Boxley. "You were a wonderful athlete. It's just that football is a game of lightning-quick reactions, and you've always been one who needs to think things through. You should've taken my advice and tried out for the bowling team."

They crossed another road, walking past the ivy-covered brick buildings of fraternity row, then entered a courtyard, at the end of which sat the Student Union Building, or SUB for short. Ethan was now looking upon the very place where he had first laid eyes on his beautiful bride.

He stopped at the door and took a deep breath. "Okay, Pinky. You and Digs wait here. We'll be right back."

"I'll stay with them," said Big. "This is not for me. It is for your family."

"But you are part of the family, Big," said Catherine.

"I'll wait here," she insisted.

"Me too," said the professor. "You guys go ahead. This is your moment."

"Okay," said Ethan. "Thanks."

Even though he and Olivia had been married for seventeen years, Ethan felt the need to check his hair in the reflection of the window. He dragged his fingers across his tongue and pushed down on a cowlick with absolutely no success. Giving up, he took another deep breath and opened the door. As much as he wanted to rush inside and scoop up Olivia in his arms, he held the door for the children to go ahead.

The first time Ethan had met Olivia it had been during a student dance, and the place was dark, noisy, and packed with people. Now, as Ethan stepped in, he saw that it was bright, quiet, and empty, except for one person. That one person was the janitor, listlessly sweeping the floor.

"She's not here," said Catherine, carefully scanning the room, though it would be hard to miss somebody in such a rectangular room and in broad daylight. "Why is she not here?"

"Maybe she's late," said Simon.

"Your mother's never late," said Ethan, his heart sinking to the floor, in danger of being swept up by the janitor.

"You're right," said a voice from behind them. Not since the Bolshoi ballet last performed *Swan Lake* had a group of people spun around so quickly in unison. There she stood near the door to the restroom, her long auburn hair gleaming in the summer sun that poured in through the skylight directly above her. She smiled and looked at her watch. "But you're twenty minutes late." Then she began to cry.

Ethan and the children rushed to her and nearly suffocated her with hugs. "What's wrong?" asked Ethan. "Why are you crying?"

Olivia shook her head. "When I woke up this morning and you were gone, I thought I might never see you again," she said between sobs of joy and relief. "And when I got here and the place was empty, I started to think the worst."

"But I promised you we'd be back before we left this morning," said Ethan. He blinked hard and gave his head a shake. "Wait a minute. What did I just say?"

It was then he realized that, not only did he remember everything that had happened over the last two years after Olivia's death, he also remembered something new—every occurrence over the two years after they had saved her life. For an entire two-year period, he and the children had lived two lives at once, and had full memory of each. They remembered Captain Jibby and his crew, the witch hunters, Sullivan and his Neanderthal wife, and the T. rex named Trixie. But they also remembered life on the run with both their mother and father, including many narrow escapes and several near-death encounters of their own. In two years' time they had experienced four years of living.

"It worked," said Catherine. "We're us again. And we're all together."

And together is how they walked out of the SUB and into the warm glow of summer, where Big, the professor, Pinky, and Digs were waiting and were overjoyed to see Olivia with them. "I told you it would work out," said Big as the smiling girl wrapped her arms around Jason's neck.

Pinky ran to Olivia, and Olivia bent down to greet the dog with a scratch behind the ears. "You know, I think I like you even better without hair, Pinky," she said. "It'll make it easier to keep the house clean."

Pinky responded with a low, steady growl.

"Uh-oh," said Catherine. "Pinky senses danger. We'd better get out of here."

Pinky snarled and barked and seemed to be directing her hostilities toward Olivia's purse.

"Mom, there's something in your purse," said Jason, snatching it away from her.

"Careful," said Catherine.

Jason moved away from the others and turned his back to them, using his body to shield them from any possible explosions. Slowly, he unclasped the purse and opened it. He peered inside and chuckled at what he saw. "Pinky wasn't growling at danger," he said, turning back toward the group. "She was growling at this." He reached in and pulled out a brand-new, freshly knitted sock puppet named Steve.

"You finished it!" Simon squealed with delight. "I knew you would." He ran to Jason and snatched the puppet from his brother. He slipped it onto his right hand and gave it a try.

"Hey, everybody, I'm back," squeaked Steve.

Everyone but Pinky gave Steve a warm welcome upon his return to the land of the living. Even Gravy-Face Roy seemed to embrace the puppet he had once seen as an adversary.

It was then that Olivia noticed the old man standing nearby. "Is that . . . Professor Boxley?" she said.

"Olivia," he responded with a smile. "It's so good to see you again."

"I haven't seen you since graduation," she said, greeting the professor with a warm hug.

"I wanted to come to your wedding, but I was accepting the Nobel Prize for physics," he replied. "Anyway, I hope you got some good use out of that lamp I sent you as a present."

"Yes," said Ethan. "We got some very good use out of it."

"I'm sorry I didn't recognize you at first," said Olivia. "It's just that you look so . . ."

"Old?" said the professor.

"That's not what I was going to say at all," said Olivia.

"It's okay," said the professor. "I'm here from fifteen years in the future, so I can understand if you thought I look older than I should."

Something suddenly occurred to Jason. "Hey, Dad— how is Professor Boxley going to get back to his own time?"

"The LVR," said Ethan.

"Are you sure?" asked Professor Boxley.

"We don't need it right now," said Ethan. "And we have the technology, so we can always build another one."

"I don't want you to build another one." Simon pouted. "Because then we'll have to go on the run again."

"I'm afraid we'll have to go on the run whether we build a new LVR or not," said Ethan. "Those people aren't going to give up until they've got the technology."

This was not at all what the children wanted to hear. This was evident by their suddenly slumping posture, which very much resembled that of their Neanderthal friends, Gurda and Stig. Ethan looked at Olivia. What kind of life had they created for their children? And could they, in good conscience, ask them to continue living such an existence?

"If they won't give up until they get it," said Simon, "then maybe we should just give it to them."

"Don't be simple," said Catherine. "Once Plexiwave gets their hands on it, there will be nothing stopping them from taking over the world. So, like it or not, we have to go back on the run."

"Well," said Ethan. "There is another option, I suppose."

"You mean we could stay and fight back?" said Jason.

"Yes, but in our own way," said Ethan. "By exposing Plexiwave for what they are and doing our best to warn others about them. We can tell our story so that no one will ever have to go through what we've had to endure."

Simon looked up at his father. "Tell our story? Wait a minute. So, are you saying . . . ?"

Ethan pulled the business card from his pocket. "That's exactly what I'm saying."

"But you told that lady that we weren't interested."

"I said you never know what the future holds. And, well, here we are in the future, with two choices. We can either change our names and go back on the run, or we can go to Hollywood."

After some consideration, Simon said, "Can we go to Hollywood *and* change our names?"

Ethan laughed and gave Simon's hair a much overdue scruffing up. "I think that's pretty much expected."

"Then call me Duke Tigerman," said Simon.

Catherine scoffed and rolled her eyes. "Duke Tigerman? Really?"

"I'm sorry," said Olivia, "but what's this all about?"

"Central Studios," said Jason. "They want to make a story about our lives. Or at least they did two years ago."

"Well, that explains this," said Olivia. She reached into her pocket and pulled out a business card identical to Ethan's. "I found this on the windshield of the car this morning. Apparently they're still interested."

"Yes!" said Jason, with an enthusiastic pump of his fist. "So what do you say, Mom? Can we go?"

Olivia pursed her lips, narrowed her eyes, and tried to imagine what life in Hollywood might be like for the Cheeseman family. Under normal circumstances, she would be vehemently opposed to the idea. But circumstances had been nowhere close to normal for a very long time. "Well," she said, "we *are* just about out of money. And I'm as tired of running as you guys are. But if we do this, our lives could end up being crazy in a completely different way."

"I'm okay with that," said Catherine.

"Me too," said Jason. "Wow, I hope they get a really famous actor to play me."

"I hope they get a really famous sock to play me," said Steve.

While the Cheeseman children were beside themselves with excitement, the significance of all this was entirely lost on Big. "I don't understand," she said. "What's a Holly-wood? And what is a movie?"

"I'll tell you all about it on the way," said Jason. Then something occurred to him that hadn't before, and his heart skipped a beat. "You *are* coming with us, aren't you?"

Big chuckled and shook her head. "Considering I've followed you through time and space, do you really need to ask?"

"No," said Jason, his heart returning to a steady rhythm. "I guess not. But I wanted to be sure, that's all."

"Okay, gang," said Ethan. "We've got a long drive ahead of us, so we'd better get moving."

"Dad?" asked Duke Tigerman with a tug on Ethan's shirtsleeve. "Before we go to Hollywood, can we go for ice cream? Like we used to?"

Ethan looked at his watch. "Well, I don't know," he said. "It *is* getting kind of late. I think maybe we should . . ."

"We should go for ice cream," said Olivia. "It's about time we did something normal for a change."

"You're right," Ethan agreed. "We should go for ice cream."

"Yes!" said Simon. "I want chocolate flavor."

"I want bubble-gum flavor," said Steve.

"I want gravy flavor," said Gravy-Face Roy.

"That's disgusting," said Catherine.

"I wonder if that place we used to go to by the physics lab is still here," said Ethan.

"There's only one way to find out," said Olivia. "Professor? Would you like to join us?"

"I would be honored," said Professor Boxley.

Ethan took Olivia's hand in his, Jason held tightly to Big's, and Catherine put aside her contempt for filthy socks and grasped her little brother's hand. If their anatomy had permitted them to do so, it's quite certain that Pinky and

Digs would also have held hands as the group made its way across campus. Professor Boxley had no hand to hold, but he was happy nonetheless, just to be in the presence of such a fine group of human beings, on their way to get chocolate, bubble-gum, and gravy-flavored ice cream.

And that, my friends, is the end of the story.

ABOUT THE AUTHOR

Due to a remarkable physical resemblance, Dr. Cuthbert Soup is often mistaken for the acclaimed writer Gerry Swallow, who began his career as a stand-up comic, making numerous appearances on *The Tonight Show with Jay Leno.* Dr. Soup's doppelgänger then turned his attention to writing movies, including the blockbuster hit *Ice Age: The Meltdown.*

Other than the aforementioned uncanny likeness, Dr. Soup has absolutely nothing else in common with Mr. Swallow, who lives with his wife and children in a very tiny mansion, whereas Dr. Soup lives in a huge mansion with his dog, Kevin, his pet snails, Gooey and Squishy, and his parents, Filbert and Roberta Soup.

Mr. Cheeseman

and his three attractive, polite, relatively
odor-free children are on the run. From what?

Well, that's a whole nother story. . . .

"If you take yourself very seriously, perhaps
this isn't the book for you. But if you're in the mood
for a lot of silliness and reading about a really interesting
and quirky family, then it's perfect."
—Wired.com/GeekDad

www.awholenotherbook.com

www.bloomsbury.com
www.facebook.com/BloomsburyKids